templar

For Emma Goldhawk,
editor extraordinaire, with thanks

A TEMPLAR BOOK
First published in the UK in 2013 by Templar Publishing,
an imprint of The Templar Company Limited,
Deepdene Lodge, Deepdene Avenue, Dorking, Surrey,
RH5 4AT, UK
www.templarco.co.uk

Copyright © 2013 by C. J. Busby
Illustrations copyright © 2013 by David Wyatt

First UK edition

1 3 5 7 9 10 8 6 4 2

ISBN 978-1-84877-939-6

MIX
Paper from
responsible sources
FSC
www.fsc.org   FSC® C020471

Printed and bound by CPI Group
(UK) Ltd, Croydon, CR0 4YY

Contents

A Lesson with Merlin

Max Pendragon was standing quite still, pinned into the corner of a plainly furnished chamber in Castle Camelot by a large, fire-breathing hell hound. Max could feel the hot breath of the dog scorching his knees, and could see the saliva dripping from its fangs onto the wide oak floorboards. It tensed its muscles, back legs ready to spring, preparing to launch itself towards him and tear his throat out.

Max gulped. Slowly, carefully, he stretched out his hand towards the hound.

"Begone!" he croaked, in what was meant to be a commanding voice but failed utterly. The hell hound bared its teeth and looked like it was laughing. Then it sprang.

Max panicked, and flung every spell he could think of at the beast, with a few random bits of raw magic thrown in for good measure. The hound turned purple, sprouted chicken wings, choked on the sudden growth of hair from its fangs, looked startled, then vanished with a loud POP!

"Well done, Max, well done," said Merlin, as he rose up from the plain wooden chair he'd been sitting in near the window. "A bit of a lack of finesse at the end there, but effective. Very effective. You're getting much stronger."

Max let out a deep breath, then slid down the wall until he was sitting on the floor. His legs didn't feel like they could hold him up any longer.

"What – what was that thing?" he said, faintly.

"Oh, you know. Guardian spell. You activated it when you opened that little box " He gestured at a small wooden casket Max was holding. "An illusion, of course, not a real hell hound. But it would have done a fair bit of damage if you hadn't dismissed it. Now Can you tell me who made the spell?"

Max groaned. Merlin had been trying to get him to identify spells for what felt like weeks now, and he was still rubbish at it. He could feel the presence of magic, but working out who had cast a spell just by the feel of it was a bit like trying to work out who had made the sword Merlin usually wore. To Max, it was just a sword – plain, workmanlike, sharp – it matched Merlin's dark tunic and weather-beaten face and made him look every inch an ordinary knight. But now that Max was better at sensing the presence of magic, he wondered how he could ever have thought Merlin looked just like any other of King Arthur's knights. Magic shone from Merlin like the fierce reflection of sunlight on water, with all the raw power of a hunting kestrel.

Max stopped short. That was it. Merlin's magic –

there was something wild about it, something that soared, that felt fierce and proud and free, like a bird. And now he realised that, he also realised something about the hell hound he'd just faced.

"It was your spell. You cast it. It felt like... like you."

Merlin clapped his hands, and grinned.

"At last, young Pendragon! At last! Yes, that was one of my earlier spells, when I was still inclined to be a bit flashy... King Uther wanted that box kept very safe at the time. Nothing much in it now, of course – take a look."

Max looked down at the open box he was still clutching in his left hand. It was ornately carved and lined with velvet. Inside was a plain gold ring. Max picked it up, and knew at once that it was enchanted. There was power in it, but it was not like Merlin's. Where his was bright and pure, and somehow felt like open air, this was dark and cold and immovable, and very, very strong. Its strength was like the strength of iron, hard and unyielding. In fact, Max felt sure he'd come up against this feeling of immovable strength before. But *where*?

He hesitated, and then put the ring on. Immediately

he felt like he'd been buried under a ton of earth. He couldn't move a muscle, although he realised thankfully a few seconds later that he *could* breathe. But otherwise the cold, hard power of the spell held him completely, so that he couldn't even speak.

Merlin looked at him sympathetically.

"Well then, Max. How about this one? Do you recognise it? Can you throw it off?"

Max tried to raise an eyebrow, or twitch the corner of his mouth ruefully to indicate that no, he really didn't have a clue, and no, he couldn't do anything about it, and could he *please* be released as he had a terrible itch on his upper arm. But it was useless, because all he did was continue to sit in the same position, looking faintly surprised.

After what seemed like an age, Merlin relented, and gestured at Max with the long brown fingers of one hand. The spell lifted, and Max sat up, relieved, and took the ring off.

"So. Did you feel the difference in that magic?" asked Merlin.

Max nodded. "But I don't know whose it is. I have no idea."

Merlin looked at him intently. "Do you remember trying to reverse your icespell from the castle two weeks ago?"

Max coloured. He remembered it very well. Having accidentally encased the whole of Camelot in a mountain of ice, it was not something he was going to forget in a hurry. Especially as his spell had got tangled up with one of Lady Morgana le Fay's, meaning it had been impossible for him to reverse it. Max remembered the panic he'd felt as he'd pushed at the icespell, trying desperately to unravel it, only to meet a cold, hard wall of resistance. A wall which, now he came to think about it, had also felt very like dark, unyielding iron...

"It's Morgana's! The spell on the ring! It feels exactly the same... *That's* why I couldn't undo it!"

Merlin nodded, delighted, and clapped Max on the shoulder.

"Well done, Max. Well done!" he said. "It is indeed

one of Morgana's favourite immobility spells. You've got it at last. You are really feeling the difference in magics."

Max felt a wave of relief. He had been wondering whether he would ever get there, and worried that Merlin might just decide he was talentless after all and give up on teaching him. But now he'd worked out what Merlin was looking for, Max realised he'd always been able to sense that shape and character to spells – he'd just never associated it with the person who made them. Now he thought about it, it made sense. His mother, Lady Griselda, made colourful, bright spells like summer flowers. Lancelot, who had helped them when they were up against Lady Morgana's plotting in Gore, made beautiful silvery spells, intricate and ornate. And the magic he had felt in Annwn, the Otherworld, had been twisted and strange, like the shadows thrown by moonlight.

Max took a deep breath, and nodded.

"Yes. I think I've got it. I can see what you mean, now. But I'm not sure how it helps."

"It's essential," said Merlin, sternly. "I need you to get a feel for Morgana's magic, especially, if you're to learn how to reverse it. And I need you to be able to reverse it if you're to help me defeat her."

Max swallowed. Help defeat Morgana le Fay, the most powerful sorceress in the kingdom? Just the memory of the powerful magic she'd used to send his sister Olivia to the Otherworld made him feel faint. And how could *Merlin* possibly need any help from him?

But before Merlin could explain any further, there was a fierce knock at the door, and almost immediately it opened. Max scrambled to his feet, and bowed. The determined-looking man who had just burst into the room was the king.

"Merlin," he said, with a nod to Max. "We have had news. Sir Boris thinks he has found the refuge of this sorceress we've been having so much trouble with."

Merlin glanced at Max. They both knew who had really been behind all the trouble the king spoke of. Morgana would stop at nothing to get rid of Arthur so that she could be queen. Together with her loyal allies, Sir Richard Hogsbottom and his son, Snotty, she had already cooked up three plots against King Arthur, and had very nearly succeeded in killing him twice. But the king would not hear a word against his sister, and instead believed it was all the work of a unknown sorceress. Catching Merlin's look, Arthur frowned.

"Merlin," he said, warningly, and his blue eyes were stern. "I know your doubts. But we are agreed that it could not have been Morgana who cast the icespell on Camelot. There is a scheming enchantress out there somewhere, and I want her found. I need you to go and join Sir Boris, find out what is going on. You will leave at once."

Merlin held Arthur's gaze for a moment, but the king was unmoved, and finally the wizard nodded.

"I will go, my lord, of course."

Arthur clapped him on the shoulder and left. Merlin sighed.

"It is a trick. They have deceived Sir Boris, they want me out of the way. But I will have to go.

Which means I need you, Max, and the others, to be my eyes and ears while I am gone."

Max nodded solemnly. They knew that Morgana was plotting something, because she had been overheard talking to Sir Richard Hogsbottom about a mysterious swordspell, a spell that would finally see the end of Arthur, and make her queen. The plot almost certainly involved the Festival of Chivalry, but so far they hadn't been able to find out anything more, and the festival was taking place in only two days. It was a terrible time for Merlin to be called away.

However, as Merlin strapped on his sword and wrapped his travelling cloak around himself, he seemed to become more cheerful.

"You know, Max, it occurs to me that this might not be such a bad thing. With me gone, they may be less vigilant. You may actually be able to find out what they are planning. I will leave you a couple of swifts, so you can let me know what you find out... Maybe this is the breakthrough we were waiting for."

As he pulled on his boots, there was a sudden

commotion outside. Merlin turned to the tall narrow window and peered out, then grinned.

"Ah," he said, and his grey eyes were sparkling with amusement. "It seems your sister has just made some equally significant progress. If I'm not mistaken, that's Mordred yelling his head off, and it looks like Olivia may have unhorsed him."

Plans and Plots

Olivia was triumphant. Jousting was not normally one of the activities novice squires were expected to learn, and it wasn't included in the Squires' Challenge, the competition she was training for. However, the sword master, Sir Gareth, was mad keen on the joust and took every opportunity to organise the squires into a mock tournament. So far, all of these had been won by Mordred of Orkney. Although still officially a novice squire, Mordred had been unofficially handling a lance since he was old enough to get on a horse – one of the many privileges of being the son of King Lot of Orkney. That he was a prince was something Mordred rarely let the other novices forget, lording it over them with his Scottish red hair and long royal nose. Now, however, his hair was streaked with mud and the back of his tunic looked like he'd taken a bath in a swamp, because Olivia had managed to push him off his horse right at the bit of the squires' training ground where the kitchen staff generally chucked their slop buckets.

The rest of the novice squires were standing around trying not to laugh as Mordred staggered upright, rubbing his head, his face nearly the same colour as his hair. Apart from a few cronies, Mordred was not liked – he threw his weight around too much, and bullied the younger ones. He had bullied Olivia when they first met over the summer at Castle Gore, until she got fed up and landed a hefty punch on his princely nose. After that they had been deadly rivals.

The other novices were secretly laying bets on which of the two would win the Squires' Challenge. Olivia was a better rider, fearless in swordplay, and a fair shot with a bow and arrow – but Mordred was twice as heavy, twice as mean, and had considerably more experience.

As Olivia cantered to a halt by the knot of watching squires, she noticed a tall, rather disreputable-looking knight standing among them, laughing loudly and waving a tankard of ale.

"Nice fall there, Mordred," he shouted across the training ground to where the muddy squire was standing in the slops. "Elegant. Masterful. Been practising that, have you?"

Mordred looked extremely put out as he tramped over to them. He scowled at Olivia, and then flung his mud-spattered hair out of his eyes and looked up at the knight.

"Push off, Gawaine," he said, coldly. "I can't even keep count of the number of times you've fallen off *your* horse."

"Ah, but never in a joust, little brother," said Gawaine,

tapping the side of his long nose meaningfully. "Only on occasions of slight... well... excess celebration."

Mordred snorted, and looked at Gawaine's tankard. "And what's the celebration for this time, then? Finally managing to get out of bed?"

Gawaine laughed, and Olivia felt herself smiling as well. She had never met Mordred's older brother, but she'd heard he was coming down for the festival, and assumed he'd be a rather sour, older version of Mordred himself. But Sir Gawaine couldn't have been more different. He had slightly straggly dark hair, blue eyes, and a three-day growth of beard. Olivia thought he looked rather like a younger, more carefree King Arthur.

"Been practising for the Knight Who Can Quaff the Most Ale in a Single Swallow," he said, holding up his tankard with a grin. "Can't let Sir Bertram Pendragon hold the honours forever," he added, and winked at Olivia, who felt herself blush.

"Nice riding," he grinned, nodding at her in approval. "And a nifty bit of work with that lance. It's not easy to unseat Mordred, he's as heavy as a sack of turnips."

Olivia laughed, and Gawaine clapped her on the back. "That's better. Well done, anyway. Looking forward to seeing you in the Challenge."

He raised an arm to Mordred, who scowled. Then Gawaine headed cheerfully back to the castle just as Sir Gareth bustled over and ordered them all to clear up and get the horses stabled before sundown.

***

As Olivia finished rubbing down her horse, a slight figure with messy brown hair slipped quietly into the stables. The rest of the squires were long gone – anxious to get up to the castle before all the food had been eaten – and only Olivia and her pet dragon, Adolphus, were still in there. Adolphus immediately bounded up to the newcomer and waved his forked tail enthusiastically.

"Did you see, Max? Did you see Olivia push Mordred off his horse? Smack! Into the mud! It was amazing!"

Max grinned, and thumped Olivia on the arm.

"I did see it, Adolphus. Very impressive."

A large black rat poked its head out of Max's tunic, and nodded to Olivia.

"Yes, excellent!" the rat said. "A dose of mud was just what Mordred needed. Pity coating your opponent in slime isn't one of the tasks set for the Squires' Challenge, or you'd win for sure."

Olivia gave her horse a last pat, then sat down on a bale of straw, looking despondent.

"The thing is, Ferocious" she said to the rat, "it was great knocking Mordred off his horse, obviously. But it made me realise just how much I really, *really* want to be a knight. And I don't think I've got a hope of winning the Challenge. It was just luck today — generally Mordred beats me at almost every task. I can't bear it – if I don't win the Challenge, Dad won't let me train to be a knight, and I'll have to go back to being a *lady*!" And she sniffed dolefully.

Max patted her on the back, and sat down next to her on the straw bale.

"Don't worry, Olivia. You're really good – everyone

can see that. We'll find a way around it if you lose."

"Yes, yes!" said Adolphus, nudging her with his long dragon nose. "Don't be sad, Olivia. Or I might start to cry..."

"And we all know where that will lead," said Ferocious darkly. "Everyone drowned in a lake of dragon tears – you definitely won't get to be a knight then."

Olivia sniffed, and grinned weakly.

"That's better," said Max encouragingly. "And anyway, it's not just the Squires' Challenge that we need to worry about. We've still got to find out what Morgana's planning for the Festival of Chivalry. Merlin's had to leave – he's been sent away to the south by the king. And he thinks we might have more chance of finding out on our own, while he's gone."

Olivia considered. "We might. And there's Lancelot, as well – he's back tomorrow from a bardic competition in Tintagel."

Max brightened. It was good to know Lancelot would be there to help them. Lancelot was one of Merlin's trusted allies. At the moment, he was in disguise as a travelling bard named Caradoc, but in reality, he was a knight, and something of a wizard too. He had been quite useful in Gore, helping them unravel one of Morgana's previous plots.

"Excellent," said Max. "Between us, we should be able to keep an eye on Morgana, and Sir Richard, and Snotty, and see what they get up to. I've been thinking about it. Our best bet is to stake out her rooms in the north tower. Ferocious has discovered a gap in the tower roof – just by Morgana's chimney – and I've made up some new frogspell potion and some antidote, just for you."

Olivia wrinkled her nose. "What, so we have to spy as frogs? I really hate being a frog."

"Tough," said Max, waving the two bottles of potion he'd just extracted from his belt pouch. "The hole is very conveniently frog-sized, and it's no good clambering around on the roof as a person, you'll get spotted instantly. Ferocious and I are planning to watch Morgana tonight, but you'll have to take over for the morning. You'll need this to transform, because

I'm not doing the frogspell on you – I'm going to be catching up on sleep."

Olivia looked mutinous. "I can't do tomorrow morning. I have a very important appointment with the practice dummy."

"Well, there's no option, sorry. Lancelot won't be here till tomorrow afternoon, and there's no one else – you'll have to."

"But it's my last chance to get my disarming technique perfected before I have to fight Mordred," wailed Olivia. "And you *promised* you'd let me fight against you afterwards, so you can't do it either."

"I'll do it!" said Adolphus eagerly, bouncing up to them. "I like being a frog! I'll watch down the chimney, I know I can be *really* quiet!"

Olivia and Max exchanged glances. Adolphus? In an important position of trust? Where he had to be really, really secret? Putting the dimmest dragon in the kingdom in charge of spying on Morgana le Fay was probably not the best idea...

"Quack! I'll do it! Quack! Always glad to be

of service!" A small duck flew down from the roof beams where he'd been watching them, and winked one beady black eye at Adolphus. "You can help me, Adolphus, if you like. Good to have a faithful follower."

"Vortigern!" said Max. "Brilliant! I was wondering where you'd got to."

The duck bobbed his head at them all in greeting, and they bowed back. They had met him a few weeks ago, when Camelot got iced, and he had been a huge help in saving the castle. He was, strictly speaking, a royal duck, after a favour one of his ancestors had done for a king, but he graciously allowed them to call him by his name rather than Your Royal Highness.

Olivia clapped her hands. "Excellent. Vortigern can keep Adolphus company. They'll be fine together, and we can all meet back here at lunch time and see what they've found out."

"Nothing, I expect," said Ferocious cheerfully. "His Royal Duckness will be too busy looking to see if they've got any bread, and Adolphus wouldn't recognise a plot if it jumped out of a bush and bit him on the nose."

But Ferocious was wrong. By lunchtime next day it had become clear that Morgana's plot involved a spell so huge that even Adolphus on a bad day couldn't miss it.

Casting the Swordspell

Sir Richard Hogsbottom was hunched over a flickering fire in the corner of a richly furnished room in the north tower of the castle. A small black cauldron was perched on the fire in front of him, and the spicy smell of magic was filling the chamber.

Sir Richard was trying very hard not to sneeze. He was aware of the dark figure of Lady Morgana le Fay close by, her long white fingers gesturing over the cauldron and her black hair snaking out around her cold pale face. Sir Richard was quite sure that sneezing, at this precise moment of magical creation, would ruin the spell and ensure that he ended his days buried under twenty feet of horse manure. But the spicy magic smell was tickling his nose and throat, and he really thought he might choke to death if he didn't at least cough. He shifted slightly in his chair, and the third figure in the room turned to him with a frown. It was his son, Adrian, otherwise known as Snotty — a tall boy of about twelve with spiky black hair. He gave his father a stern look, then turned back to the cauldron, passing Morgana a small glass bottle.

"Hair from the head of Arthur Pendragon," said Morgana with satisfaction, and cast the contents into the pot. The liquid inside bubbled, turned a deep green colour and gave off a smell of newly mown grass. Snotty passed her another bottle, again containing a lock of hair, and she added it with a twisted smile and a comment about the knight it belonged to, but Sir Richard was not paying attention. He was pinching his nose tightly between his finger and thumb and holding his breath, trying desperately not to release the sneeze that was now forcing its way up through his whole body.

Morgana passed her hands over the cauldron and closed her pale blue eyes, concentrating hard. In her low, honey-sweet voice, she chanted the words of the spell, and tendrils of golden yellow steam started to rise up from the surface of the liquid, which was slowly changing colour. Snotty, too, seemed to be holding his breath, but more from awe than the need to keep down any kind of inappropriate snort. Sir Richard thought he really might die if he didn't sneeze this instant, and for a moment wondered if either of his two companions would actually care.

He contemplated them both through watering eyes. This was the fourth time they had come together in a plot against King Arthur, but so far each of those plots had been foiled by that dratted boy Max Pendragon and his dreadful sister Olivia, along with their ridiculous pet rat and dozy dragon. To say nothing of their utterly ghastly father, Sir Bertram.

At the thought of Sir Bertram Pendragon and his ridiculous moustache, Sir Richard sniffed hard. Unfortunately, the sniff met the sneeze somewhere round the back of his throat, and that was that. Sir Richard exploded in a shower of spit, snot and pent-up snort that was so sudden it didn't even have time to sound like a sneeze, more like the last yell of a dying man. Which it very nearly was.

Luckily for Sir Richard, at exactly the same moment as the sneeze Morgana lifted up her white arms and spoke the final words of the spell. The whole room seemed to shiver, and a burst of light from the cauldron seared Sir Richard's eyeballs. When he could see again, Morgana was holding a shining sword with a gleaming jewelled hilt, and was shaking the last drops of potion off its length.

"The swordspell," she breathed. "The final spell. The spell that will bring Arthur Pendragon down."

She turned her icy stare on Sir Richard, and her expression would have frozen the heart of the bravest knight. Not being the slightest bit brave, Sir Richard quaked, and waited for her to blast him down into the castle duck pond with a swift transference spell. But Morgana had not noticed his sneeze. She had been too intent on the magic in front of her.

"So, Sir Richard," she said, and smiled at last. "The first part of the plan is in place. A few more easy little spells and then we have him. And I..." she took a deep breath, and raised the sword aloft, "I shall be queen... at last!" Her expression was triumphant, and terrible. Sir Richard could not suppress a shiver, but Snotty smiled, and the expression on his pale face was an almost exact mirror of Morgana's own.

***

Down in the castle practice yard, Max was flat out on the ground, looking white, and Olivia was hovering over him, wringing her hands.

"Max, I'm really sorry — are you all right? I thought you'd dodge it... I didn't mean—"

"Well that's all right then," said a sarcastic voice. Ferocious slid out of Max's belt pouch, wincing, and sprawled on the ground next to him. "Didn't *mean* to kill

31

us both with your ill-timed thrust to the midriff... So we'll just die here quietly and you can put flowers on our grave to show how sorry you are. Charmed, I'm sure."

Max groaned, and Olivia knelt down beside him, looking concerned.

"Max! Are you all right?"

"Uurrghh..." was all he could manage, but there was a little colour coming back into his cheeks, and he seemed to be breathing again. After a few minutes, he opened his eyes, and gingerly sat up.

"Druid's toenails!" he gasped. "What *was* that?"

"It was a disarming manoeuvre Dad showed me yesterday," said Olivia, looking guilty. "I thought you knew it was coming. I thought you'd dodge it."

"No," said Max, with a dismissive wave of his hand. "Not you. Just before you whacked me – there was something... like a rock fall. The whole castle shook."

Olivia looked puzzled. "I didn't notice anything. Are you sure?"

"Ferocious? Did you feel anything?" asked Max.

"Nope," said Ferocious, shaking his head. "Nothing I could feel. Sure it's not the knock on the head, Max? Or... well... I know it's a bit embarrassing to get defeated by your little sister but, you know, she's getting very good. You don't need an excuse for going down to her savage disarming technique."

Max frowned. "Very funny, Ferocious. But I felt something massively powerful hit me. And if none of you noticed it, it makes me wonder if it was something to do with magic."

"But there's magic going on all the time, Max," said Olivia. "All sorts of spells and enchantments all over the castle. They don't normally affect you."

"It's true, they don't," said Max, thoughtfully. "But maybe — if it was a really massive spell..."

Olivia frowned. "You think it might be Morgana? You think it might be this swordspell she's been planning?"

At that moment there was a loud squawk and a clatter, and a small flapping duck crash-landed right in the middle of them and started quacking really loudly. He was followed by Adolphus, who collapsed in a tangle of limbs and wings and tail, snorting fire and gulping in panic.

"Feel that?! Sent my feathers standing on end! Feel like I got struck by lightning! Quack! Shock of my life!"

"Yes!" gulped the dragon. "A big bang! Help! Olivia! Max! It was fire... and lightning and... and... I don't feel very well." And Adolphus rolled over and shut his eyes.

"Vortigern!" said Max. "What happened?"

"We were at the top of the north tower," said the duck, shaking his wings and waggling his head as if he were trying to get water out of his ears. "Watching down the hole. Couldn't see much — she was brewing a spell. And then... Hit me like a boulder to the head. Can't stand up straight." And indeed, he was weaving slightly from side to side as he tried to get all his feathers back in order.

"You can feel magic, can't you?" said Max thoughtfully. "You've always says it makes your feathers go tingly."

"Hah!" said the duck, his beady eyes looking slightly crossed. "Tingly feathers! More like my insides got skewered by a red-hot poker! And the blast of it took the frogspell off us both in a second. I tell you, after all that I really need a bit of bread. Quack!"

Max reached into his belt pouch, where there was always a stray bit of breakfast, and handed Vortigern a crust of bread, which he started to gobble happily. After a couple of minutes, the duck looked up.

"The thing is," he said, "just after the blast, before we scarpered, we saw what she was holding up. It was a *sword*."

"Yes, yes," said Adolphus, raising his head slightly and thumping his tail. "She had a big sword. A really shiny big sword."

"Max!" said Olivia. "That sounds like..."

He nodded. They must have done the swordspell. The spell that Morgana had said would sort out King Arthur once and for all.

"It's obviously something really big," said Max, with a shiver. "I need to send a swift to Merlin, right now."

Max is Stuck

Ten minutes later, back in his chamber, Max finished writing his message to Merlin. Carefully, he spoke the words that turned the creamy white parchment into a small fluttering white bird, ready to fly to wherever Merlin was to be found. But as he let the swift go out of his window he spotted Snotty Hogsbottom, looking furtive, entering the castle at a small side door near the eastern wing. As quickly as he could Max hurried after him, and was soon tiptoeing quietly along one of the darker and more remote corridors in the eastern part of Castle Camelot. He was almost close enough to sense the faint buzz of magic that always accompanied Snotty, who never went anywhere without a belt pouch full of potions and spell powders, when suddenly there was a clatter ahead and a curse.

"Dragon's breath, Jerome! You're such a clumsy oaf!"

Dungballs. Snotty obviously had Jerome Stodmarsh with him. Jerome was Sir Richard Hogsbottom's ward and Snotty's faithful sidekick, a large meaty boy with red hair and a nose like a pig. Max slipped into an alcove. He had no great desire to be caught following Snotty, and he was even less keen to have to face Snotty and Jerome together.

There was a scuffle further along the corridor and then Jerome's voice, whining.

"Why do we always have to do the dirty work?

We've spent hours trying to get into his chambers without being seen. I'm meant to be practising for the archery contest. Why can't your father slip it into his wine?'

"Do try not to be as stupid as you look, Jerome," came Snotty's drawl. "A potion isn't strong enough. It's got to be in his clothes. Father can't get near enough, anyway. They don't exactly get on, in case you hadn't noticed."

Max wondered who they were talking about. They were going to enchant a knight, that was clear, slipping the spell into his rooms, which must be near here. The trouble was, most of the knights here for the tournament had been given chambers in the east wing. Unless Max could get closer, and actually see which room they went into, he would be none the wiser. He had just started to creep towards the edge of the alcove, when there was a sudden yelp from Jerome, and a hiss from Snotty.

Max froze. Heavy footsteps were coming up the corridor from the other end, and he could hear the clang of armour, and raised voices. He strained to make out who it was from the voices, but the knights were all talking at once, great gusts of laughter mingling with shouts and claps on the back. After a while they clearly turned down another corridor and the noises faded away.

"Now!" Snotty hissed. "His chamber's free. Come on, Jerome, you great slug. It's our best chance!"

Max carefully peered round the edge of the alcove, just in time to see Jerome disappearing into a knight's chamber. He crept quietly towards the door, hoping to see whose rooms they were sneaking into, but before he got within twenty feet there was a nasty laugh from behind him. Max's heart sank.

"Oh dear, Pendragon. Not very clever. Did you really think I wouldn't stay back and keep a look out for any nosy spies happening to stroll past? Not much brighter than your sister's dozy dragon, eh?"

Before Max could even turn round, Snotty flicked a few drops of liquid at him from a bottle he was carrying, and Max fell to the ground like a marble statue. Snotty pulled a rough, smelly sack over Max's head, and a few minutes later Max felt himself being hauled painfully along a twisting, turning route, up some narrow stairs, and out onto the castle battlements.

"Now, Pendragon," came Snotty's sneering voice, as they dropped him roughly on the ground. "Much as I'd love to dump you over the battlements into the moat, Lady Morgana doesn't want *any* kind of trouble to disrupt the festival, and finding your immobilised body floating face up in the moat might cause a few awkward questions. So I'll just leave you here where you'll be nice and cold and hungry for a few hours. Teach you to stick your nose in where it's not wanted!"

He pulled the sack off, and Max could see that he was at the furthest corner of the most remote part of the castle battlements, stuck behind a pile of old stones and beams that had been used to repair one of the turrets. The spell on him wouldn't wear off for hours, and meanwhile he couldn't move or utter a word. He couldn't even make a face at Snotty, who was grinning down at him with one eyebrow raised.

"Nothing to say, Pendragon? Ah well. Enjoy

your afternoon!" And he and Jerome sauntered off, leaving Max fuming.

***

It was nearly nightfall before the others managed to find Max. He had spent hours trying to undo the immobility spell that Snotty had cast on him. He could tell it was Morgana's magic — it felt like cold iron bands were wrapped around him, holding him tight. Every attempt that Max made to unravel or throw the magic off just seemed to pull it tighter around him. In fact, he was pretty sure that the spell would have worn off much quicker if he'd just left it alone.

By the time Ferocious came scampering out onto the battlements, Max could just about raise one eyebrow and make a soft whistling noise.

"Ah," said Ferocious, when he'd tracked down the strange noise to the pile of stones in the corner. "Here you are. I'm guessing you ran into our old friend Snotty?"

Max tried to nod, but didn't succeed. He rolled one eye instead.

"Right then," said the rat, nudging his ear in a friendly fashion. "I'll just go and get the others."

When the rest of them came clattering up the winding stairs a few minutes later, Max was half glad, half dismayed to see that Merlin was with them. Merlin seemed weary, and his clothes were spattered with mud. He looked as if he'd been travelling hard, and in his hand was Max's swift. Lancelot bounded up the stairs behind him, and when he saw Max his long crooked face broke into a grin.

"Dear, dear. Caught by one of Morgana's special little immobility spells, eh? Happens to the best of us. I spent a few hours propped up in the corner of her chambers, once. She used me as a hat stand."

Olivia stifled a laugh, then tried to look solemn and concerned, while Merlin reached over and wafted the spell off Max with a wave of his hand. Max sat up stiffly, and rubbed his elbow where a stone had been digging into it.

"I tried to take it off," he said, defensively. "I really did. It just seemed to bind it tighter."

"Really?" said Merlin, raising his eyebrows and looking pleased. "That's actually a good sign. You were getting hold of the magic, at least. But Morgana's magic is tricky. It can get you turned around if you're not careful, not paying attention. You can end up adding your magic to hers, rather than undoing it. But you've done well – it's the first stage. You just need to practise more."

He threw Max a small grey stone, and Max fumbled, dropped it and then scrabbled around on the ground. Olivia sighed, and picked it up for him.

"It's bespelled," said Merlin. "Morgana had an argument with Sir Peverell at a feast a few years back and stormed out after turning the entire banquet into a small pebble."

Max looked at the stone in his hand. He could feel the iron touch of Morgana's magic – but a whole feast? In one small pebble?

Merlin smiled. "Keep it, Max. See if you can take it off. Your reward will be roast boar's head and more cinnamon pastries than you could eat in a month.

But more than that," he added, more seriously. "I feel we are coming to the end, with Morgana. And I need you to help me, Max, to defeat her. Which means you *must* be able to overcome her spells. So — practise!"

Max looked up at Merlin, who was looking back at him intently. He thought of Morgana's cold expression and the terrible power of her spells, and his legs felt like straw — but then he met Merlin's bright, fierce eyes and took a deep breath, and nodded.

"I'll do my best," he said. "But I'm not sure why you need my help."

Merlin frowned. "I can reverse any spell she cares to throw at me, but as for defeating her... She has been getting more powerful, and it's been clear for some time that she can undo my spells. I cannot defeat her alone. But together we have more of a chance." He clapped Max on the shoulder and smiled. "You have more power than you realise, Max. When the time comes, you'll be ready, I know it."

He looked round at the others, then rubbed his hands together. "Well, this battlement seems as good a place as any for a council. But I'm ravenous!" He gestured at the ground, and food and drink appeared on a rug nearby. Adolphus whooped, and got stuck in to a large bowl of woodlice.

Merlin lowered himself to the rug and helped himself to a large piece of chicken.

"So," he said thoughtfully. "We know Morgana has done her swordspell. But do we know anything else about it? Max? Could you tell anything from the feel of it?"

"Only that it was powerful," said Max, reaching for a pastry. He thought back to the tremor that had run through the whole castle. It had hardly felt like a spell, more like a huge landslide thundering down a mountain. Now he thought about it, though, there had been the cold feel of Morgana's magic at the heart of it. And something else – something he'd felt before...

"It was Morgana's spell – but there was something mixed up with it. A different magic."

Merlin leant forward eagerly. "What did it feel like? Did you manage to recognise it?"

Max tried to concentrate on the memory – but it had all happened so fast. There was something about the other magic in the spell – something familiar – but he just couldn't put his finger on it. He sighed.

"Sorry – I don't know. Maybe Vortigern felt it?"

They turned to the duck, who quickly swallowed a large piece of bread and bobbed his head.

"Quack! The spell nearly blew all my feathers off. I couldn't tell one end of it from another. Quack! But we did see them put some hair in it. Hair from the head of Arthur Pendragon, and then hair from another knight – but I didn't catch the name. Got a bit of soot in my ear. Adolphus? Did you hear who it was?"

He turned to the dragon, who thumped his tail eagerly on the ground.

"Yes – I know! It was... um... Sir Bors... No – it was Sir Edgar... Or – was it – um – no! Oh! I'll get it in a minute, I know it, I do really!" He closed his eyes in fierce concentration and put his clawed feet over his head, muttering to himself.

Merlin turned to the others.

"Let's assume this knight is supposed to wield the magical sword she's made. Who is fighting the king in the tournament tomorrow?"

"I am," said Lancelot, unexpectedly. "If I get through to the final. At the moment I'm in the other half of the draw."

Merlin raised his eyebrows. "So. Decided to reveal yourself as a knight, Lancelot? And are you entering with your own name?"

Lancelot grinned. "Well, no. I'm planning to keep my helmet on, so no one will know who I am. I'm just down as the Knight of the Lake."

Olivia's eyes shone. She was already looking forward to seeing King Arthur fight – now she would get to see Lancelot as well. Merlin had once told them that Lancelot was the best knight he'd ever seen. Maybe he would even be a match for Arthur himself. But then Arthur had Excalibur, so that made him pretty much invincible. Unless...

"Merlin!" she said. "You don't think... Excalibur... Could Morgana have done anything to Excalibur?"

Merlin shook his head. "No. Excalibur's safe.

It's bound to Arthur by the magic of the Lady. No other knight can even wield it without that spell being remade. Morgana couldn't begin to attempt magic as deep as that." But his face looked troubled, and he rubbed his chin with his hands thoughtfully. "Morgana's magic has been getting stronger, I've felt it. It's still no match for the Lady's, but it's possible she has managed to make a very powerful magic sword."

At that moment Adolphus suddenly leaped up with a cry.

"Got it!" he said eagerly. "I've remembered! It was King Arthur! She put King Arthur's hair in the spell!"

They all looked at each other, and Ferocious rolled his eyes.

"We know that, pea brain," he said. "It was the *other* knight we wanted you to remember."

"Oh," said Adolphus, crestfallen. "Oh, well, *that* was Gawaine."

"Gawaine?" said Olivia, startled. "Mordred's brother? But he can't be in on the plot! He doesn't seem like the sort to be in with Morgana!"

"Um, well, then maybe it was Gaheris," said Adolphus, confused. "Or – Gareth... Something beginning with 'G' anyway."

"Snotty was down by the knights' chambers," said Max thoughtfully. "It sounded like he was planting a spell, but he could have been taking the sword down there as well. And Arthur will be fighting Gawaine in the tournament. Although he'll also be fighting Sir Gaheris *and* Sir Gareth..."

There was silence, as they all tried to work out what Morgana was up to. At last Lancelot spoke, slowly.

"Arthur will be seeking only to disarm his opponents in the tournament – it's supposed to be just a friendly test of skills. If this other knight – Gawaine or whoever – wields a powerful magic sword, and is aiming to kill the king, then Arthur could be in danger. Even with Excalibur. He could be killed before he realises the fight is to the death."

Merlin nodded, and then sighed. "I shall warn the king. I don't have much hope that he will withdraw from the tournament. Still – I will enhance his shield with magical protection, it should be enough to hold against Morgana's spelled sword, keep him safe. But we must all be on our guard. There's something about the plot that worries me. Something we're not seeing... I don't like it."

Max looked at Merlin. His magic should easily be a match for Morgana's. But the wizard still seemed anxious. Max exchanged glances with Olivia. So far, they had always managed to foil Morgana's plots and save the king. What if this time they couldn't? What if this time, she actually succeeded?

King Arthur
is Warned

A small finger of sunlight pushed through a gap in the tapestries draped across Max's window. Gradually it lengthened, and traced a path across the dark floor towards Max's bed, until finally it brushed across his face and poked him brightly in the eye.

Max flinched and flung his arm up over his face, then he opened his eyes. For a moment he couldn't remember where he was or what had been happening. Then he heard the peal of several hunting horns outside, the jingle of horses' harnesses and the shouts and calls of a gathering of riders. It was the Veterans' Hunt, the traditional early morning start to the Festival of Chivalry. That meant there were only two hours before the first events of the Squires' Challenge, and after that, the real business of the competition – the single combat for the Knights' Cup. In which King Arthur, as reigning champion, would have to meet any knight who was called against him in the draw.

Defeating the challengers for the Knights' Cup had never been a problem for King Arthur up to now. But that was before Morgana le Fay had created the most powerful spell she'd ever made, and provided one of his opponents with a magic sword. One of the knights in the festival had been primed by Morgana to fight the king to the death and they had to hope Merlin's shield would hold against her spell or the king was doomed.

Max sat up and swung his legs over the edge of the bed. As he did so, there was a clatter on the floor.

A small grey pebble had fallen off the blanket where he'd left it the night before. Morgana's pebble.

Idly Max picked up the stone and began to feel for the magic in it. He pushed against the hard iron wall of the spell, wondering how he was ever going to break it. And then he thought about Merlin's words. Morgana's magic was tricky, it turned you around so you added your own magic to the spell, rather than reversing it. Max stopped pushing against the enchantment and held still, just feeling it at the edge of his consciousness. Gradually he became aware that there was a background of magic around it, like a huge dark absence of anything – and suddenly he realised that this was where the power was. Not in the cold, hard, unyielding wall of iron but in the dark absence around it. He felt his way into the absence, beginning to pool his own magic inside it, trying to dissolve it. With a growing sense of excitement he felt the stone grow warm in his hand. Could he smell roasted meat?

At that moment the door to his chamber burst open and Olivia came rushing in.

"Max! It's the festival! It's now! It's today! I can't do it – I'm going to fail!"

Adolphus flew in behind her in an equal flap, careened right into a roof beam and crash-landed on Max's head.

The pebble reverted instantly to a cold, dark grey stone. Max, almost completely engulfed by the sprawling dragon, kicked his legs and gurgled frantically. One kick managed to make contact with Adolphus's head, and Adolphus flopped off the bed onto the floor, where he lay feebly coughing.

"Druid's toenails, Adolphus!" said Max, taking a great gasp of air into his lungs. "You nearly suffocated me!"

Ferocious, who was perched on top of a nearby chest washing his whiskers, snorted.

"It's your own fault. If I were as much of a lazy slug as you are, Max, Adolphus would have landed on me, too, and I'd currently be squashed as flat as a fetching rat-shaped tapestry. Were you planning on getting up at all this morning?"

Max made a face and heaved himself off the bed, swiftly pulling on some leggings and a tunic and running a hand through his messy hair.

"Right then. Breakfast."

"I can't eat anything!" wailed Olivia. "It's the competition in less than two hours! I've got to saddle a horse and arm a knight faster than any of the other squires. And before that I have to hit the bull's eye in the archery target and knock down the dummy with a well-aimed saddlebag. And if that wasn't enough – this afternoon I have to beat Mordred in a sword fight! Max – I need some magic! I need you to spell my bow so it shoots straight! I need you to—"

"Calm down. It's going to be all right," said Max soothingly. "You'll be fine. You're really good at throwing the saddlebag – and you're quite good at archery. Who are you arming?"

"Dad," groaned Olivia. "And he's twice as large as most of the other knights, so he has twice as many bits of armour. Plus he's ticklish, so he's always wriggling. So far I've come last every time we've practised."

Max tried not to laugh, because Olivia was so distraught – but it was hard to keep a straight face at the thought of her dressing their father in all his many bits of armour while he danced around trying to avoid being tickled.

"I'm sure he'll behave for the actual competition," he tried to reassure her. "Come on – come and have something to eat. Lancelot might be down there, and he can tell us if Merlin had any luck with the king."

***

As it happened, Merlin was still with the king, and he was not having any luck at all.

"Merlin, I cannot withdraw from the competition. Are you mad? I am the king! I cannot look like a coward."

Merlin sighed. "I thought you would see it that way. Well, at least let me put some extra protection on your shield. And you must take great care – there may be one knight in the competition aiming to kill rather than disarm you. Be aware of the danger."

Arthur smiled, his blue eyes clear and unafraid.

"I can defend myself, Merlin. And even if there is some magic sword being wielded against me, I have Excalibur! What can go wrong?"

Merlin nodded, and then frowned. "Where is Excalibur, though? You don't have it with you."

"No," said Arthur. "It's with Morgana. She wanted to add some protections of her own before the tournament — she was worried about this rogue sorceress."

Merlin looked startled. "You have given it to Morgana? But, my lord... did she have it yesterday? If the spell we felt was carried out on Excalibur..."

Arthur held up his hand. "Enough, Merlin! That spell had nothing to do with either Excalibur or Morgana. I trust her. She is my sister."

Merlin stood for a moment, hesitating, but Arthur raised his blue eyes to Merlin's grey ones, and held his gaze.

"If I cannot trust Morgana with my life," he said, and suddenly he sounded unbearably weary, "then perhaps I would rather not live."

Merlin sighed, and nodded.

"So be it, my lord," he said. He bowed, and left the room.

After Merlin had gone, Arthur took a deep breath and rubbed his hands over his face, and wondered if he had done the right thing.

***

"Olivia! Olivia for the Challenge!"

Max was shouting as loudly as he could but he was drowned out by the roar of Sir Bertram beside him.

"That's my girl! Show them what you're made of!"

Sir Bertram had waxed and curled his enormously magnificent moustache in honour of the festival. With his large frame and deep voice, he was attracting more than his fair share of attention from the surrounding crowd. He and Max were sitting at the front of the tiered seating which had been arranged around the castle green. Filling the seats were countless knights, ladies, children, witches and wizards in brightly coloured clothing and there was an air of excited anticipation. Sir Bertram was trying to forget that he was already in terrible trouble with his lady wife Griselda for letting Olivia even enter the Squires' Challenge, and would be in even deeper trouble if she won. He couldn't help secretly hoping she'd actually make it. She really was a fantastic squire, and would make a very decent knight. Sir Bertram could see it now – setting off on quests with Olivia at his side. The Knight with the Most Magnificent Moustache and The Only Knight Who Is a Girl. What a pair they'd make!

Olivia, pale but determined, stepped out into the middle of the castle green with the other squires, her bow in her hand. Adolphus, next to Max, couldn't stop bouncing, and had already nearly singed Sir Bertram's moustache with a bit of over-excited fire-breathing. Ferocious was perched on Max's shoulder, cleaning his whiskers, and Max could just see Vortigern waddling in front of the crowd further on, catching the bits of bread people were throwing to him.

There was a drum roll, and gradually an expectant silence fell over the crowd. The castle sword master, Sir Gareth, strode out with the archery target and set it up a hundred paces from the nervous bunch of squires.

"Our first contestant," he bellowed, "is Geraint Muddpuddle of Castle Caerleon."

A thin boy with bright blonde hair stepped forward, and drew his bow almost before anyone had time to clap. His arrow whistled across the green and struck the target just off-centre. The crowd cheered and stamped their feet. The Squires' Challenge was a popular event – a good-humoured extra alongside the real business of the festival and a way to spot upcoming talent. Quite a few people staked bets on the winners, and Max could see money changing hands in the crowd as people reassessed Geraint Muddpuddle's chances.

As the next contestant took his place in the centre, Lancelot slipped quietly into the seat next to Max.

"Olivia next, then," he said with a wink, and showed his fingers crossed. "I've got five gold pieces on her to win."

"Five?!" said Max. "Are you sure?"

Lancelot tapped his finger against his nose and

winked again. "I've seen her in action," he said. "She's got some very special disarming techniques."

Sir Bertram heard, and grinned. "Excellent. Excellent. I've got a bet on her too, as it happens. And a trick or two up my sleeve. Just wait and see."

A Fight to the Death

At that moment, the sword master called Olivia to the middle, and she walked out, looking very small and rather white. There was a slight buzz of surprise and discussion – she was, after all, the only girl ever to have entered the competition – and then a good-humoured cheer.

Olivia squinted at the target. There was the slightest breath of wind, and she adjusted her aim carefully

to take account of it. Then she drew her bow and loosed the arrow in one smooth fluid motion. The bow twanged, and the next second the arrow had thudded into the target – right in the bullseye. The crowd roared, and Sir Bertram whooped and clapped Lancelot on the back, sending him pitching forward into the barrier in front of them.

Unfortunately for Olivia, Mordred also managed a bullseye – so they were in joint first place at the start of the next event: Knock Down the Dummy with a Well-Aimed Saddlebag. Olivia was pretty good at this – but Mordred was bigger and heavier, and could throw a saddlebag that Olivia couldn't even pick up, so he won by a mile.

The final event of the morning was Prepare and Arm Your Knight. Max almost couldn't bear to watch as he saw Olivia lined up with the other squires, each with their knight and horse. Mordred was arming Gawaine, who was slim and supple, and looked as if he could shrug himself into his armour with almost no help. Sir Bertram, on the other hand, was large, heavy and ponderous, and his old-fashioned armour had several fiddly fastenings that needed a great deal of pulling and pushing to get around his ample frame. The horses might even things up a bit – Sir Gawaine's looked like a temperamental charger, while Sir Bertram's horse, Daisy, was a docile old nag, quite happy to stand still for hours. But Max didn't think it would be enough.

Olivia looked despondent, but Sir Bertram, strangely, was trying very hard not to grin. He leant sideways and murmured in her ear.

"Cheer up, Olivia! Got some new armour as a present from your mother last week. Wasn't going to get it out in the practice runs – didn't want the opposition to be put on their guard. But we're going to win this one, my dear girl. We're definitely going to win!"

Olivia looked down at the pile of armour, startled. It was indeed a whole new suit. And there seemed to be far fewer pieces to fasten together... She looked up at Sir Bertram, suddenly hopeful. He winked.

"Easy-fastening buckles," he said triumphantly.

"And it all fits beautifully. No pulling or pushing required."

The horn sounded, then a drum roll, and then Sir Gareth roared, "Arm your knight!" The centre of the green instantly turned into a frenzy of clashing, clanging armour, squirming knights, panting squires and stamping horses. But in the middle of it all, Max could see Sir Bertram disappearing under shining bits of metal faster that he'd ever thought possible, and Daisy happily standing still as a statue while Olivia flung on her harness and saddle.

Meanwhile Sir Gawaine's horse was snorting and stamping and flinging his head around while Mordred cursed. Gawaine stood quite still and blank beside him. Odd, thought Max, that he was neither helping nor laughing, nor indeed doing anything much at all. It wasn't like Sir Gawaine. But as he turned to nudge Lancelot and point this out, the horn sounded to mark the end of the event, and Sir Gareth announced with a great shout:

"Olivia Pendragon wins the third event! Mordred of Orkney second! And Geraint Muddpuddle third!"

***

Olivia's triumph with Sir Bertram's new armour put her in very close second place overall, just behind Mordred. Everything now depended on the single-combat event in the afternoon. But before that was the first round of the Knight's Cup, where King Arthur was scheduled to fight three bouts, against Sir Gawaine, Sir Lionel and then Sir Gaheris. Lancelot had told Max and Olivia of Merlin's unsuccessful attempt to warn the king, and Max could see Merlin himself, standing at the other end of the ground, looking grim. There was an air of huge expectation in the crowd – after the fun of the Squires' Challenge, this was a more serious business. Lady Morgana le Fay was sitting up high in the Royal Box, overseeing the event, with other knights and ladies around her. Max spotted Sir Richard Hogsbottom pouring her a glass of wine – and making some toadying compliment, no doubt.

The first knight to face Arthur would be Sir Gawaine.

"I can't believe Gawaine would be working for

Morgana," said Olivia. "He's just not evil enough."

Max nodded. "Maybe. But there was something odd about the way he was behaving in the Arm Your Knight event. He wasn't helping Mordred much."

"I'm not sure Gawaine likes him," said Olivia. "Another point in Gawaine's favour, as far as I'm concerned."

A hush fell over the crowd as the two knights strode to the middle of the green and saluted each other. King Arthur's sword shone in the afternoon sunlight, looking just as impressive and glorious as ever. Gawaine's, on the other hand, just looked like an ordinary weapon. Would he be wielding Morgana's bespelled sword, or was it one of the other knights? Max could see Merlin, frowning intently at both swords, and Max wondered if he'd felt any magic when the knights had raised them to each other.

He tried to feel for the magic himself. There *was* a definite whiff of Morgana's magic in the air, but also a bright magic that felt like the clear water of a bubbling stream, a magic that felt vaguely familiar...

Max suddenly realised where he'd felt that magic before – in the potion the Lady of the Island had given him to dissolve Morgana's icespell. And not just there – he'd also felt it yesterday. The other magic that he'd sensed, the magic that had been mixed in with Morgana's spell – it was the Lady's magic! No wonder it had felt familiar. But that meant...

"Olivia!" he hissed. "The spell yesterday! It was the Lady's magic that was mixed up in it! And the Lady's magic is what bound Excalibur to Arthur. Morgana must have been doing her spell on *Excalibur*! She wasn't making a new sword – she was unbinding the Lady's magic so someone other than King Arthur could wield Excalibur! You were right!"

"But – Merlin said she wasn't strong enough!"

"But he also said she's been getting more powerful. Somehow she managed to undo the Lady's binding – and then she must have changed the swords' appearance and swapped them! It's not Arthur that's got Excalibur – it's Gawaine!"

The two knights were circling each other, both with

their helmets fully closed, swords at the ready, shields up. Each had already tried a few feints, probing the other, but so far neither had struck seriously. Then King Arthur, so fast that Max barely had time to follow it, darted under Gawaine's guard and struck a blow on his leg. Gawaine stumbled, and Arthur was on him, but Gawaine managed to raise his shield, and Arthur's sword glanced off. As he recovered Gawaine struck a glancing blow on Arthur's own shield, and it buckled.

The crowd gasped. Lancelot frowned, and rose to his feet. Arthur's shield was enhanced with Merlin's magic – surely no sword of Morgana's could have broken through Merlin's spell so easily? But as the sword came flashing down, Max had felt the singing power of the Lady's magic.

"Gawaine's got Excalibur!" he shouted to Lancelot. "Someone's got to stop the fight! Arthur's in terrible danger!"

"He's going to kill the king!" said Olivia. "Max! We've got to *do* something!"

Before Max could say anything she had vaulted

over the barrier and was running onto the ground. Max followed, with Lancelot beside him, taking great long strides towards the king. On the other side of the green Max could see Merlin, who had obviously realised what had happened at exactly the same time as they had, running towards the knights and shouting, in his commanding voice, "Stop! Stop the fight!"

But they were too slow, too far away.

Arthur seemed to have realised that he was fighting against Excalibur. He was defending himself desperately, but Gawaine was strong and fast and clever, and he had the most powerful magical sword in the kingdom. Gawaine had Arthur on the ground, now, his shield shattered. He raised Excalibur with both hands, and, just as Merlin roared, "No!" he brought it down and plunged it into Arthur's chest.

There was a moment of utter stillness. Then Gawaine pulled out the sword, and fell to his knees. There was a scream in the crowd. Max and Olivia stood where they were, unable to move. They felt like they had been turned to heavy stone. Tears were streaming down Olivia's face. Many in the crowd had covered their faces with their hands. Lancelot suddenly looked ten years older, the bones of his long face prominent, his skin grey. They all watched as Merlin walked slowly across the ground towards the fallen body of the king. Gawaine was still kneeling nearby, his helmet removed, his hair dark with sweat, his face revealing no emotion.

"The king is dead!" came a cry from the crowd. Morgana stood up tall in the Royal Box, her dark hair falling around her white shoulders, her face a mask of apparent shock and grief.

"My dear brother," she cried. "Arthur is dead..."

"And you, his loyal sister," said Sir Richard Hogsbottom reverently, down on one knee, "You are now our queen!"

But Merlin was now in the centre of the green, gently starting to remove Arthur's armour. Suddenly he halted, and his eyes widened. He ripped off Arthur's breastplate, and then one armguard, and then he started to unlace the rest of the armour as fast as possible. Max and Olivia craned forward, unable to believe what they were seeing. The whole crowd seemed stunned – but eventually it was impossible not to accept what had happened.

Merlin stood, a mixture of relief and shock on his face.

"The king is not dead!" he announced. "The king has... vanished."

The Quest to Find the King

The mood in the castle that evening was sombre. A great feast had been prepared to celebrate the end of the festival but right now no one was quite clear whether they should be celebrating or mourning. Was a vanished king better than a dead king? Would Arthur return, or had he been dispatched to the Otherworld, never to be seen again? Was Morgana le Fay now their queen, or was she simply a temporary regent? King Arthur's senior knights had been gathered with Lady Morgana for most of the afternoon, trying to decide what to do, but no one had heard from them yet.

Olivia and Max were glumly sharing a large pie and a pile of pastries near the end of one of the long banquet tables. Under the table, Adolphus was finishing off the scraps Olivia threw to him, and Vortigern was halfway through a pile of bread somewhat larger than himself.

"Well, all I can say is, I hope they string Gawaine up by his toenails," said Olivia, savagely stabbing her knife into a piece of meat. "I can't believe I actually liked him!"

Ferocious, sitting on Max's shoulder, rolled his eyes. "We've been through this. He was obviously enchanted. You only had to look at him."

"Yes – enchanted. Or doing a good job of pretending to be," said Max, thoughtfully. "After all – he *is* Morgana's nephew. Like Mordred."

Olivia muttered something into her pastry that sounded like 'Stinking slime-covered pile of rat's droppings', but at that moment the great door at the end of the hall opened and Morgana le Fay entered majestically, with Arthur's knights around her, all looking grim.

Sir Bertram spotted them and came over.

"We're going on a quest," he said, as he reached them. "Groups of two knights and two squires, to search for Arthur. Three days to find him, or news of him, and after that, if there's no success, we make Morgana queen." He sat down heavily. "Bad business, really bad. But if we can't get Arthur back, there's no help for it. The kingdom needs a ruler."

"So that's you and me, then, one knight and one squire for the quest," said Olivia, in a tone that made it clear she would not take no for an answer. "And Max may have taken up magic, but he's a squire as well. We just need one more knight."

Lancelot, who had been sitting silently on Max's other side, raised his head.

"Well I think that had better be me. It's time for me to be a knight again."

Sir Bertram raised his eyebrows. "A knight? Are you really? Splendid! So, I suppose Caradoc isn't your real name then?"

Lancelot bowed his head to Sir Bertram, and gave a wry grin. "My true name is Sir Lancelot du Lac. At your service, Sir Bertram."

Sir Bertram bowed back, and clapped him on the shoulder.

"Well, good to have you along, Sir Lancelot. I'll let Lady Morgana know."

"Me too!" came an eager voice from under the table. "I want to come!"

"Yes, yes," said Olivia soothingly. "Of course we'll be taking you, Adolphus. And Ferocious."

"Quack! And me! Won't get far without me!" said Vortigern, flapping onto the table. "Need a royal leader, after all!"

Lancelot laughed. "Well – it's supposed to be only two knights and two squires, but there's nothing to say how many animals you're allowed to take. I guess that means we're all going!"

"Good," said Sir Bertram. "We'll make our preparations and be off at first light."

* * *

The castle yard was grey and chilly in the light of dawn, full of stamping horses and men in jangling armour. Morgana had come to see the knights off, and wish them well on the quest. They were to reassemble in three days, and if there was no news of Arthur they would assume him lost forever. Max could see her discussing something in low tones with Sir Richard Hogsbottom, who was leading one of the search parties. Beside him was Snotty, and the other knight of their group was...

"Olivia!" said Max, grabbing her by the arm. "Is that Gawaine?!"

She narrowed her eyes, and then nodded.

"What's he doing here? He should be in the dungeons!"

"It seems he was under an enchantment," said Sir Bertram. "Can't be blamed. Lady Morgana took it off him, and he said he wanted to join the search — help as much as he could. The knights have agreed he can take Excalibur along to give back to Arthur if he finds him."

Max watched Gawaine, standing blankly by his horse.

"It doesn't look much like she took the enchantment off," he said. "He still looks thoroughly enchanted to me."

"I think so too," said a voice nearby, and they turned to see Merlin, who had quietly joined them in the castle yard.

"Merlin!" said Max. "What's been happening? Are you coming with us?"

Merlin grimaced. "I can't. I need to stay here and keep an eye on Morgana. I underestimated her badly, it seems, and I need to be ready for any other plans she might have. But there is another reason." He lowered his voice. "Max, I am pretty sure Arthur has gone to the Lady. Morgana was not powerful enough to completely remove the magic that bound Excalibur to Arthur. In the end the sword would not kill him – I think it sent him to her, wounded, no doubt, but alive. It is there you will

79

find him. But I cannot come with you. I promised the Lady a while ago that the next time I set foot on her island it would be to stay for good."

"For good? But you can't!" said Max, shocked.

"Indeed," said Merlin, rather sadly. "I am needed too much here. But one day..."

There was a faraway look in his eyes, and Max got the impression that for Merlin, staying on the Lady's island for good would be like a clear draught of water to a thirsty man.

"Max! Olivia! Time to go!" said Sir Bertram, leading up the horses. Merlin leaned urgently in to Max.

"The Lady's island is not where you saw it last. It moves. And it's tricky to find, you need to look beyond the surface of things. And be ready for whatever challenges may come. Use this –" He handed Max a small silver ring. "It is a gift from her. It will pull you towards the island. Of course, Sir Richard and Sir Gawaine will be on your tail. They have Excalibur's magic to guide them. And if they get to Arthur first, he will not return alive."

Max nodded, and pocketed the ring. As Max mounted his horse, Merlin also handed a small folded piece of parchment up to him.

"A swift," he said, in a low voice. "Send it to me if you have great need. And keep your wits about you!"

He smiled then, and held Max's gaze.

"You can do it, you and Olivia and the others. I know you can. Take care!"

There was a loud peal from the royal hunting horn, and the gathering of knights raised their swords in the air and shouted, "For Arthur!" before they set off in a great stream of horses and men and squires, across the drawbridge and out into the kingdom on their quest for the king.

***

Within a very short time, the crowd of knights that had left Camelot had dispersed in different directions, and Sir Bertram's little troop found themselves ambling alone along a leafy green lane, the sky bright blue behind the trees and a gentle breeze encouraging the leaves to dance and twist in the branches overhead. Every time the road forked or met a crossroads, Max could feel the faintest tug from the ring on his finger, pointing them in the right direction.

He was feeling quietly optimistic. They knew where they were going, and the Lady would keep Arthur safe till they got there. They had three whole days before they had to get back to Camelot. Surely that would be enough time?

There was a squeal from overhead, and Adolphus very nearly knocked Max off his horse. He and Vortigern were having a flying competition, dodging in and out of the beeches that lined the road. They were seeing who could fly through the most trees while breaking off the least number of branches. So far, Adolphus, being quite a bit larger and clumsier, was down by forty-two branches to Vortigern's none, and Max wondered with a grin whose idea the competition had been.

"Whoopee! One more!" cried Adolphus as he flew straight into a beech and a great limb of the tree came crashing down onto the path ahead of them.

"Adolphus!" said Olivia crossly, dismounting to clear the branch out of the way. "You're supposed to be trying *not* to knock the branches off!"

"Oh, sorry, am I?" said Adolphus. "Oops! I'll be more careful!"

Ferocious groaned. "Will someone please just turn them both into frogs and stuff them in a saddlebag?"

Lancelot laughed. "Oh, leave them alone, Ferocious. We could do with a bit of entertainment. Take our minds off whatever Morgana le Fay has in store for us — if we actually succeed in the quest.

Max looked over at Lancelot. Despite the danger they were in he thought that he had never seen Lancelot look happier. Perhaps it was because he was allowed to be himself at last — a real knight. He seemed completely at home in his armour, his sword by his side, his eyes bright and alert in his crooked face.

At that moment, there was a crash and a splintering sound in the trees ahead, and the next second a huge knight in black armour came charging out of the woods and pointed his lance at them.

"Halt! I challenge all who pass! Fight me, strange knights, if you wish to continue!"

"Quack!" yelped Vortigern, who had almost flown straight into the sharp end of the stranger's lance, while Adolphus did a triple somersault and landed in a heap in front of the black knight's horse.

Fights and Magic

"**O**h, I say – is that Adolphus?" said the knight, and raised his visor for a better look.

"Flame and thunder!" exclaimed Sir Bertram. "Peverell! What are you doing here?"

"Bertie!" shouted the strange knight, and he lowered his lance and cantered forward. "What a jolly surprise! On a quest, eh? What's it all about?"

It seemed as good an excuse as any to stop for lunch, and Sir Bertram invited his old friend to join them while he explained what had happened at Camelot. Several meat pies and a few bottles of mead later, Sir Peverell gave a mighty burp and thanked them for the meal.

"Terrible business about the king," he said, pulling his beard thoughtfully. "Don't want that awful le Fay woman running things. Disaster. You'd best get on with your quest. But before you go, I'm afraid I really do have to joust one of you. Made a vow, you see. Can't get out of it."

"That's okay, quite understand," said Sir Bertram. "I'll have to borrow one of your lances, though, didn't bring my own."

"Actually, I would enjoy the honour, if I may," said Lancelot, and stood up in one smooth motion, bouncing on the balls of his feet and looking quite eager to take the lance Sir Peverell was holding out. Max exchanged glances with Olivia. They both felt quite excited at the idea of seeing Lancelot in action. It would be a treat to see him joust Sir Peverell, who was renowned as a hard man to unseat.

Sir Peverell bowed, and went to his horse.

He lowered his visor and cantered back a good distance along the path, then turned, ready. Lancelot mounted, holding the lance he'd been given, then tried the grip in a few different places, getting it nicely balanced.

"At your service, Sir Peverell," he called, and lowered his visor.

The two knights started towards each other, slowly at first and then with more pace, their lances held out in front of them. Olivia watched, excited, as the horses gathered speed and the lances hurtled ever closer to impact. At the last minute Max couldn't help flinching and shutting his eyes. There was an enormous crash, and when he opened them again Sir Peverell was on the ground, bouncing along on his bottom, while Lancelot wheeled his horse round to canter back. Olivia, Adolphus and Vortigern were cheering loudly, while Sir Bertram had gone to help his friend up.

"I'm fine, Bertie, fine... Fine," he groaned. "Nice work, young man. I'll be sure to add you to the roll of honour back at the castle. What was the name? Sir Lancelot?"

Lancelot nodded, looking pleased.

"Good, good. Excellent. Well – nice meeting you all. Good luck on the quest! Let me know if you survive!"

They waved cheerily at Sir Peverell as they headed on, and Sir Bertram entertained them for most of the afternoon with tales of the mischief he and Sir Peverell had got up to in their youth. One particular escapade had involved a bad-tempered dragon, a hoard of gold, and Lady Griselda, who, it appeared, had rescued both of them from the dragon at the last minute with a nifty dab of magic.

"Of course, we both wanted to marry her after that," said Sir Bertram happily. "But she said I was the man for her. The moustache, you know." He stroked it, proudly. "Always did impress the ladies."

Lancelot raised one eyebrow, and Olivia nearly choked from laughing, but Sir Bertram just grinned. "Well, whatever it was, jolly glad she chose me. Fine woman, your mother. Fine woman."

Eventually it started to get dark, and when they reached an open expanse of moor by a small stream it seemed a good place to camp for the night. They gathered firewood, and Adolphus set it aflame with a single snort. Soon the horses were unsaddled, and everyone was huddled round the fire together sharing out the food.

It was a relatively cheerful supper, but Max was beginning to feel a bit anxious. One whole day gone, and they seemed no nearer to finding the Lady's island. They weren't even anywhere near the sea – every time the road veered or turned towards the coast, the ring seemed to pull them back again, deeper into the countryside. Max had no idea how much longer it would take, and he was very aware that there were now only two more days before Morgana crowned herself queen.

***

The next day it rained steadily, and it was hard for any of them to keep their spirits up. The ring took them deep into what seemed like an endless forest, and after a few hours Max started to wonder whether they would ever get out or whether they were just going round and round in circles.

But it was when he ended up in the ditch that he got really angry.

He was at the front of the group, feeling his way forward, when his horse stumbled on a tree root. Max slid helplessly over the horse's neck and rolled down the sloping path, straight into a muddy ditch full of swampy, smelly water.

"Urrghh!" he spluttered, as he pulled himself upright and clambered out, spitting mud out of his mouth and shaking leaves out of his hair.

It was a measure of how gloomy they all were that no one even laughed.

"That's it!" said Max, thoroughly fed up. "I've had enough. This ring is taking us round in circles, I'm sure of it!"

Lancelot looked down at Max thoughtfully.

"Did Merlin say anything about how to see the island when we got there?"

Max considered. Merlin *had* said something. What was it? He'd said that it was tricky to find. That they'd have to look beyond the surface of things.

Max looked down at the ditch in front of him, the ditch of muddy, swampy water, and realised that there was something odd about it. He was much wetter than he should have been after falling in something only a few inches deep. Almost as if the ditch was actually bigger, deeper...

Max looked at the trees around them, and the path ahead, and tried to see what was behind them, as if they were painted scenery hiding what was real... As he did so, the trees seemed to clear like a mist, and a great dark expanse of lake opened up in front of him, with a small wooden bridge built out into the water, leading to the Lady's island.

The others gasped, and they all dismounted and started to walk forward. But as they did so five figures emerged from a path to their left and a cold sarcastic voice greeted them.

"Too late, Pendragon! We got here first."

"Snotty!" said Max, and felt for his sword. Lancelot had already drawn his, and so had Sir Bertram. Opposite them stood Snotty and his father, with Gawaine,

Mordred and Jerome Stodmarsh. But before anyone could move, a voice came from the bridge.

"Both parties arrived at the same time. Both have a different purpose. There'll have to be a competition."

A tall, thin man with mousy-brown hair and faded minstrel clothes was standing on the bridge. He was chewing a piece of straw, which he took it out of his mouth and pointed at them all.

"Each knight fights another knight, each squire fights another squire. One at a time – with no help from the others. The overall winners get to cross the bridge."

"Never mind that rubbish – we're going across now!" said Snotty, and headed onto the bridge with his sword drawn. The next second he was on his back in the mud, and his sword was back in its scabbard. The man shook his finger.

"Naughty," he said. "Knights first, squires second. Equals fight equals. When you're ready."

Max looked at the group in front of them. "There are five of them – how did they manage that? It was supposed to be two squires and two knights!"

"Rotten cheating scumbags," said Olivia darkly. "Morgana's pets, I suppose."

"Maybe Snotty hid behind Jerome when they counted," said Ferocious with a nasty grin. "He's wide enough to hide an army."

Max frowned and did a rapid calculation. "We have to fight with equals. I suppose that means Sir Richard for Dad, Gawaine for Lancelot, I'll have to fight Snotty..." he gulped, and then went on, "And Olivia, you'll have to fight Mordred. Jerome will be left over. I don't know what will happen then. Maybe four fights will be enough."

"Or I could bite his ankles till he yields," said Ferocious, showing his white teeth.

"Right, well, better get on with it," said Sir Bertram, and strode into the small clearing by the bridge without even bothering to put his helmet on. "Come on and fight, Sir Richard, like a true knight!"

Sir Richard looked like anything but a true knight, his pasty face full of horror and his sword waving around rather wildly as he inched his way towards Sir Bertram.

"I... er... well... I say... Do we have to? Really? Isn't there a more civilised way of— Ow!" He gave a great squeal as Snotty walloped him on the back and sent him flying into the clearing, where Sir Bertram immediately started laying about him with his big sword. Sir Richard managed to fend him off for a while with a combination of shield, sword and running away, but it was clear that the fight was not going to go Sir Richard's way. Until he reached into a small pouch round his neck, and threw a few grains of powder in Sir Bertram's direction.

Sir Bertram immediately found his feet stuck fast in the mud. What was worse, he was sinking into the ground, which had become extremely oozy exactly where he was standing. Sir Richard capered just out of reach of Sir Bertram's long sword, and smirked.

"Yield, Sir Bertram!" he said. "I believe I have you at my mercy!"

"Mercy? That's a good one!" roared Sir Bertram. "Stop dancing around like a girl and come a bit closer. Then I'll show you who's in need of mercy!"

But Sir Bertram was already up to his knees in

the swamp, and sinking rapidly.

"That's not *fair*," shouted Olivia. "You can't do that! Max – take the spell away!"

But Max was already trying. It was one of Morgana's, he could tell, and he was carefully concentrating on the edges and emptiness around what seemed to be the spell, trying very hard to dissolve it. But it was a slow process, and Sir Bertram was now up to his waist, waving his sword to keep Sir Richard at bay.

Desperately Max tried harder. Even though he knew where to concentrate now, it was like trying to undo a huge complicated knot. If he could just find the right bit to start pulling at, he knew it would all collapse, but so far nothing had worked.

"Yield!" said Sir Richard again, sternly, at Sir Bertram's head, the only bit of him still visible.

"Never!" said Sir Bertram, and as he said it, there was a great sucking, squelching sound and the swamp closed over the top of his hair, leaving nothing but a trail of bubbles on the surface and a few inches of sword disappearing rapidly into the gloop.

King Vortigern
the Victorious

"Dad!" shrieked Olivia, as Sir Bertram disappeared into the swamp.

But at that moment Max found the right bit of Morgana's spell and heaved with all his might. There was a loud POP and Sir Bertram shot out of the ground. He was deposited in a heap at the feet of the man on the bridge, who took his straw out of his mouth and looked down.

"You are a stubborn man, Sir Bertram," the man observed. "But you are deemed to have yielded anyway – help is not allowed from other parties. Sir Richard wins."

Sir Richard gave a slight bow to his companions, and retreated, while Sir Bertram, looking thoroughly disgruntled and extremely muddy, stumped back to the others.

"Blasted magic!" he muttered. "Not at all fair. Not allowed in a *proper* fight!"

The man on the bridge waved his piece of straw at them.

"Sir Gawaine must now fight Sir Lancelot."

"But he's got Excalibur!" said Olivia, suddenly realising. She turned to Lancelot. "You can't!"

Lancelot gave her a crooked grin. "It's okay, Olivia. I'm prepared to be beaten by the best sword in the kingdom. Although," he winked, "I have a trick or two that might just help..."

He strode into the clearing, his sword at the ready. Gawaine, looking pale and expressionless, started towards him, Excalibur drawn. Max could feel the buzz and sing of its magic, which was even stronger here, so close to its source.

The man on the bridge held out his arm, and then dropped it.

"Begin!" he said.

Lancelot moved before Max even realised the fight had started, and his sword flashed and thrust and parried so fast it looked like three swords at once. Gawaine seemed startled. He was an able swordsman, and he had the finest sword ever made, but Lancelot was like a force of nature, beating him steadily backwards. Just as Gawaine began to rally and press back at his opponent, Lancelot twisted his sword in a manoeuvre that seemed to involve him passing it from one hand to the other. Before Max could even work out what had happened, there was a flash of sunlight on metal and Excalibur was in the air, tumbling across to the other side of the clearing, while Gawaine was on his knees with Lancelot's sword at his neck.

"I yield," he said, in a dull voice, and Lancelot sheathed his sword.

"Sir Lancelot wins," announced the man on the bridge. "Now – Max Pendragon fights Adrian Hogsbottom."

**

Max knew exactly what he was going to do. He was going to turn Snotty into a frog. He had wanted to turn him into a frog ever since he had first discovered the frogspell potion, but there had never been the right opportunity. The one time he had thrown some at him in a fight, it had turned out to be harmless blackberry sludge which Olivia had swapped for the real potion. Snotty had just laughed. Now Max was going to get his revenge.

"Olivia," he hissed. "Have you still got the frogspell I gave you?"

She nodded, and fished the blue bottle out from her tunic.

"But you don't need it, Max," she said, surprised. "You can do the spell without the potion."

"I know," said Max. "But that needs concentration

— and it will take longer. If I just chuck a bit of this at him it'll all be over in a few seconds."

She passed him the bottle, carefully, and he took the stopper out and stepped into the clearing.

"Come on then, Snotty," he called. "Come and fight."

Snotty inched warily into the clearing, his eye on the potion bottle. In his hand, he had a small packet of powder. The two boys circled each other, trying to get close enough to aim their spells but watching carefully for any sign of sudden movement from their rival.

Then Max, not watching his feet, slipped on a patch of mud, and Snotty darted forward and flung the contents of the packet in Max's face. At the same moment Max flicked the bottle in his hand and a couple of lumps of blue frogspell hurtled towards Snotty. The spells hit their targets at almost exactly the same time. Snotty disappeared with a BANG and in his place was a bright green frog with clashing pink spots, who looked thoroughly disgruntled. Max, meanwhile, had keeled over sideways, stiff as a board, encased in another of Morgana's famous immobility potions.

This time, however, Max knew exactly what to do. He rapidly felt for the outside edges of Morgana's spell, and into the black absence that surrounded it. Then he grabbed hold of the very end of the magic, and pulled. Almost immediately he was free again. Before Snotty had had time to do more than croak a few times, Max had whisked him up and stuffed him into a small drawstring bag. He tied the top triumphantly, and then whirled it round in the air a few times, to make sure Snotty came out feeling thoroughly sea sick.

The man on the bridge nodded.

"Max Pendragon wins," he said. "The other contestant must now be restored to human form."

Max made a face, dropped Snotty out of the bag, and concentrated for a few seconds.

WHOOSH!

Purple stars flew around the clearing, and Snotty, looking queasy but decidedly human again, staggered back to his companions.

"Olivia Pendragon fights Mordred of Orkney," announced the man on the bridge.

Olivia swallowed hard. So far she'd never managed to beat Mordred in single combat in all the times they'd met during training. She was not very hopeful that she'd do it now, in this muddy clearing in the middle of nowhere, when so much depended on it.

Sir Bertram smacked her on the back, encouragingly.

"Don't worry, Olivia. Just do your best."

Lancelot nodded, and leaned down.

"He's bigger than you, and heavier. But you have the advantage of speed. Get in at the beginning. Get him on the run."

Olivia nodded, and took a deep breath. She unsheathed her sword, and strode into the clearing. At the other end, Mordred stalked forward, looking down his long aristocratic nose at her.

"Well, it's little Olivia Pendragon. Come to play with the big boys again? You know you haven't got a chance."

"Eat dung, Mordred," said Olivia, through gritted teeth. "Just be thankful you're not on a horse or I'd have you in the mud before you could pick your over-long royal nose."

Mordred narrowed his eyes at her. "That was a fluke, little girl. You won't do it again. In fact you won't be doing anything very much when I've finished with you."

They had gradually drawn closer as they taunted each other. Now Mordred lunged forward, his sword aimed straight at Olivia's head. She parried it smartly, and then stepped sideways, aiming a blow at his left side. But Mordred was quicker than he looked, and her sword met his shield with a clashing blow.

Max almost couldn't bear to watch. Olivia was good – much better than he'd ever seen her – and she was giving Mordred trouble. But he was just too strong. One heavy blow he landed on her shield looked like it almost shattered her arm, and she was wincing in pain as she tried to beat him back. She almost got him with a swift disarming manoeuvre but he managed to turn slightly and deflect it, and then he obviously decided he'd had enough of playing by the rules, and punched her hard on the arm. Olivia yelled, and dropped her sword, and the next second he had picked it up and was holding both swords at her neck.

"Yield!" he said.

"You cheating, evil, fat pig's backside!" spat Olivia. "That's not fair!"

"All's fair in war," said Mordred, and pressed the swords harder against her neck.

"I yield," said Olivia, with tears of rage and frustration in her eyes.

"Mordred of Orkney wins," said the man on the bridge.

Olivia stomped back to the others, cursing Mordred non-stop under her breath. Max gave her a pat on the back.

"You nearly won, you know," he said. "It's why he had to cheat, in the end."

"He's a rotten stinking troll's bogey," said Olivia angrily. "But he'd have won anyway – he just wanted to cut it short. I can't beat him! I just can't! He's too big and heavy. And that means I'm *never* going to win the

Squires' Challenge, and I know it shouldn't matter because if we don't rescue King Arthur there won't even *be* a Squires' Challenge, but I'm never going to be a knight. *Never!*" and she nearly burst into tears.

Lancelot bent down and put his arm around her and murmured in her ear. Olivia's eyes brightened.

"Really?" she said. "You promise?"

He nodded.

"Right, you're on. As soon as we've finished the quest." She seemed a whole lot happier and Max felt relieved. Whatever Lancelot had said, it had worked.

"Two wins to each side," announced the man on the bridge. "Jerome Stodmarsh may choose his opponent from the remaining members of the Pendragon party."

"Remaining members?" said Sir Bertram. "What does he mean?"

"He means me!" said Adolphus eagerly, and shot into the clearing. "I'll fight him! I've fought him before! Whoosh! I chased him away in the forest!"

"Or me," said Ferocious, scampering after him.

"I'll bite him, and then I'll bite him again. I'll bite him in places he didn't even know he had."

"Quack!" said Vortigern, flying after them. "It's me, of course. I'm the next in line. I'm a *royal* duck! Quack!"

Jerome stood on the other side of the clearing, looking completely taken aback at the idea that he was now called upon to fight. He took a quick look at the opposition and decided almost immediately.

"The duck," he said. "I'll fight the duck."

It was over in seconds. Vortigern was a small whirlwind of wings and beak and webbed feet. He smacked Jerome repeatedly around the head with his wings and pecked his ears. He dodged Jerome's flailing arms with ease, and then went back for another go, poking him in the eye with his webbed feet.

"I yield!" shouted Jerome. "I yield! I yield! Get him off me!"

Vortigern retreated to the middle of the clearing, where he strutted proudly, rearranging his feathers.

"I told you so," he quacked. "I am King Vortigern

the Sixth. Never been beaten in a fight before."

The man on the bridge waved his piece of straw at them all.

"The Pendragon party wins. They can leave their horses here safely, and proceed to the island."

He stood to one side, and gestured at the bridge. Max and the others looked at each other, and then warily stepped forward. Snotty tried to move in front of them, but he was held back, as if by an invisible wall. His face was distorted with rage as he spat at them.

"Don't think you'll get away with this! We'll be waiting for you when you come back! And not just us, either. You won't make it to Camelot, I can promise you that!"

Max stepped on to the wooden bridge, and as he did so, he felt the cool greeting of the Lady's magic. They had made it. They were on the island. But it seemed distinctly possible that the real challenge was going to be getting off it again in one piece.

The Lady's Island

The Lady was exactly as Max remembered her. She was kneeling down in the cabbage patch, with her long frizzy brown hair tied back with a colourful bit of cloth, her hands muddy and her sleeves pulled up to the elbows.

"Ah," she said when she saw them, wiping a streak of mud across her forehead as she pushed a stray bit of hair out of her eyes. "You'll be here for Arthur.

He's in there..." She gestured at the little cottage behind her. "I brought Leogrance's girl here to look after him, couldn't spare the time myself. Got the cabbages to see to."

She waved them on. "I'll be in in a minute. Go and introduce yourselves."

Lancelot bowed low to her and passed eagerly on to the cottage, the others following behind.

They had to duck through the low door, but once inside, the cottage seemed much larger than it did from the outside. A fire was burning in the grate and a pot of stew was suspended above it, bubbling gently. A wooden chair had been pulled close to the fire, and Arthur was sitting on it, looking weak but very much alive, with a small black cat purring gently at his feet.

"My lord," said Lancelot, and went down on one knee in front of the king. "We are relieved to see you well and safe."

Arthur looked at them all, their faces weary but triumphant. They had found him. They had the king back. They had succeeded in the quest!

He sighed and tried to sit more upright, grimacing slightly.

"Well done. You have found me, and I am alive — though I never expected to be. I thought I was dead when I woke up here — but then I realised that I hurt too much. I imagine that when you are dead, you don't feel anything." He smiled, and then winced. "So. I suppose I'd better see about coming back with you."

He didn't sound terribly enthusiastic about the idea. Olivia looked at him carefully. The king was pale, and clearly in pain, but there was something about him that made her think he was happier than he'd been for a long time. Lines of care and worry seemed to have been smoothed out, and his face looked much younger.

At that moment a door at the back of the room opened, and a young woman came in. Arthur looked up, and his whole face brightened.

"My nurse," he said, gesturing at the young woman. "The Lady Guinevere."

Guinevere was tall, with long nut-brown hair and eyes exactly the same shade of blue as the king.

Max thought that she was the most beautiful person he'd ever seen, but her beauty was in more than just her features – it was in the way she moved, the way she tilted her head, the hint of amusement in her eyes, and the twitch at the corner of her mouth. When she spoke, her voice was musical, and it made each one of them feel they had known her forever.

"Welcome, all of you. Please – have something to eat."

She waved, and immediately there was wine and pastries, apples and mulled mead on a table by the fire, along with roasted woodlice for Adolphus, bacon rind for Ferocious, and bread for Vortigern. Max looked up at her, startled. Was she a witch? She smiled and winked at him, and he coloured and tried to neaten his messy hair. Olivia snorted. She was the only one not charmed by Guinevere's long eyelashes and merry blue eyes. She kicked Max on the shin, in a bad temper, and sat down by the fire with a pastry.

"So," said Arthur. "Lady Guinevere – this is Sir Bertram Pendragon, and his excellent children,

Max and Olivia. The handsome duck you see over there is, I believe, King Vortigern, and his fiery companion is Adolphus. And the rat on Max's shoulder is Ferocious, who is extremely useful in a scrap. Is that everyone?"

"Not quite," said Guinevere, looking hard at Lancelot. He had been sitting in the shadows, half hidden. Now he looked up, and his crooked face was slightly stern.

"Guinevere," he said, with a nod.

She bit her lip.

"I thought so! Lancelot! What are you doing here?"

"You know each other?" said the king, surprised.

"The Lady Guinevere and I grew up together," said Lancelot. "When I left, we were not on the best of terms."

Guinevere coloured slightly.

"I threw his best sword in the moat," she said.

Arthur raised his eyebrows, and she pouted slightly.

"Well, he lost my favourite hunting hawk. And broke my harp."

"Because you left it where I would trip over it!" said Lancelot hotly. "And I never lost Gloriel, you lost him yourself!"

The two of them looked thoroughly cross with each other, and about ten years younger than they actually were.

Arthur laughed, and pulled Guinevere to him.

"I think we can agree to put this dispute behind us, can we not?" he said, smiling at them both. Guinevere hesitated, and then smiled back, and squeezed the king's hand.

"Of course," she said, and turned to Lancelot. "Sir Lancelot, I hope you can forgive me the wrong I did you. Shall we be friends?"

Lancelot took a deep breath, and nodded. "As you wish." But he remained slightly stern for the rest of the evening, and Guinevere avoided his glances.

It was much later that the Lady entered, with a gust of wind, and slammed the door behind her.

"Right then. Plans made, I take it? Worked out how you're going to get back to Camelot?"

They all looked blankly at each other. They had been too busy enjoying the fire and the food, and the feeling that everything was going to be all right now they had found the king. They hadn't begun to think about how to get back to Camelot.

The Lady looked at them all brightly, and took an apple from the bowl.

"It's just I imagine Morgana will be waiting for you on the other side of the bridge."

Arthur's face darkened.

"Morgana," he said, and for a moment all the old weariness and care was back in his face. "I was wrong about her. She was the only one who could have worked that spell on Excalibur, and then changed its form. I have been blind... Merlin was right all along."

"Oh yes," said the Lady tartly. "Of course. Merlin's *always* right." She snorted, and threw her apple core at the cat. "The question is, how are you going to get away, when he hasn't seen fit to come along and *help*? And when I can't leave the island?"

Arthur looked taken aback.

"Well, I'm not much use in a fight at the moment. And I haven't got Excalibur."

"Lancelot's a pretty nifty swordsman," said Sir Bertram, stroking his moustache. "And I'll do my best, of course. And we've got Adolphus..."

"I'll fight too!" said Olivia, fiercely. "We'll all die before we let that evil witch rule the kingdom!"

Ferocious rolled his eyes.

"Yes, well, very noble – but it would be better if we didn't actually have to die. So I suggest we pretend we didn't find the king at all, and we smuggle him back to Camelot in the saddlebags, as a frog."

Max whooped and clapped his hands.

"Genius!" he said. "That might just do it!"

"I'll need Guinevere with me," said Arthur quickly. "She's an excellent nurse, and I'm still not feeling completely healed."

"That's fine," said Olivia instantly. "Guinevere can be a frog as well. Better that way, or they'll wonder why she's with us. She'll make a *lovely* frog."

She smiled at Guinevere, and Guinevere smiled

sweetly back, but her beautiful blue eyes were narrowed.

***

Max sent his swift to Merlin later that evening. They had decided to start back for Camelot in the morning – Arthur needed another night's rest, and it was already late. No one felt like facing an ambush by Morgana in the dark.

When morning came, it was sunny, and a slight mist rose off the still waters of the lake so that it was hard to see the other end of the bridge. Sir Bertram and Lancelot were in full armour, ready for whatever awaited them, and Olivia had her sword drawn. Max had turned the king and Guinevere into frogs earlier. The king was now a large midnight-blue frog with purple spots, while Guinevere was a very fetching pink frog with long eyelashes. Both of them were carefully stowed in an old saddlebag, which was slung across Max's shoulders.

The Lady was standing by the bridge, peering across the lake.

"I can come with you to the far side" she said.

"But I can't do any magic on the shore. You'll have to hope Merlin got your swift, and that he will actually turn up."

"What about the man we met before?" said Olivia. "The one who made us fight? Where is he?"

The Lady coloured.

"He... well... um... actually – that was me. It is the rule, you know. If two groups seek entry at the same time..." she trailed off. "Anyway," she added, in a brighter tone. "You all did very well. Especially Vortigern."

"Quack!" said the duck happily. He was perched on Lancelot's shoulder, flapping his wings a bit to keep balanced. "Always glad to help. Ready to defend the king with all my might."

"And me!" said Adolphus, flying round their heads noisily. "I'll fight them! Just you watch me. And Ferocious will help too!"

"If you don't tip me off with your ridiculous flying stunts," said the rat, clinging on to Adolphus's shoulder.

"Good. Excellent. Right then," said Sir Bertram,

and gave his moustache a last twirl. "Forward, and be ready for whatever meets us!"

They strode onto the bridge, Sir Bertram first, followed by Lancelot and Olivia, with Max at the rear. The bridge seemed to expand as they stepped onto it, so that by the time they reached the shore they were more or less four abreast, with the Lady walking behind them.

As they reached the end of the bridge, they saw Snotty and Sir Richard, standing with Sir Gawaine behind them, and Mordred not far away.

"Where's the king?" said Sir Richard, looking at them hard.

"Haven't got him," said Sir Bertram airily. "He wasn't there. So you've waited here for nothing, I'm afraid. Better try somewhere else."

Sir Richard frowned, and looked taken aback. Snotty narrowed his eyes at Max.

"What are you up to, Pendragon?" he snarled. "The king was on the island. If you don't get him back to Camelot today, then he won't be king any more."

"Sorry," said Max with a shrug. "He really wasn't there. We just stayed for a chat and some roast venison. So out of our way, please – we're going home."

There was a pause, while Sir Richard and Snotty put their heads together. For a moment, Max thought they might actually get away with it. But then a voice called out of the trees. A voice that filled him with cold dread.

"He is lying. The king is with them – I can feel it. Kill them all!"

From out of the shadows stepped a tall figure – a figure with long black hair and a white face. Morgana le Fay. She had come to stop them herself.

The Battle for the Kingdom Begins

From behind Morgana, ten or twelve knights in full armour moved out of the trees, their weapons raised. Max gulped. But Sir Bertram didn't hesitate. He drew his sword, and with a cry of "Up and at 'em!" he swept off the bridge, Lancelot beside him and Olivia not far behind. There was a clashing of metal as their swords met those of the oncoming knights. Sir Richard rapidly got out of the way, but Snotty and Mordred and Gawaine joined the battle with a will.

Max hesitated, put down the saddlebag with the two frogs inside, and then drew his sword – but the Lady put her hand on his shoulder.

"I think it's your magic they'll be needing, Max, not your sword," she said gently.

He took a deep breath and nodded. There was one thing he could do to start with which would even the odds up a bit. He concentrated on Gawaine, down there in the frenzy of fighting, and felt for the enchantment he knew was binding him: Morgana's magic, stored in some small object. He was guessing it was in Gawaine's clothes somewhere, hidden there by Snotty and Jerome that day at the castle... He began to sense the magic, and started to unravel it.

***

Meanwhile, Olivia was fighting for her life. Sir Bertram and Lancelot were back to back, holding off five or six of the knights between them, while Adolphus was proving himself a useful ally, chasing at least four of Morgana's men around the clearing in circles and breathing fire at them. Ferocious, clinging on for dear life, was urging him on. Vortigern was harrying another knight mercilessly, flying into his face and repeatedly pecking him on the nose. But that still left Olivia to defend herself against Gawaine, Mordred and two other knights. This she was doing by a combination of dodging behind trees and dealing swift blows to their legs when they were least expecting it. Being shorter than everyone else was proving a distinct advantage – but it wasn't enough.

One of the knights had her cornered now, and although she was still parrying his blows bravely, she thought she probably only had a few seconds before he sliced her head off. Just as she thought this, however, there was a shout from behind her, and her opponent fell back, his shield shattered by a blow from... Excalibur!

She turned in surprise to see Gawaine's bright blue eyes regarding her with an amused expression.

"A thank you would be nice," he said, with a grin.

"But... what?! You were on the other side a minute ago!"

His face darkened, and he frowned.

"I'm not sure what's been going on," he said. "I can't remember much. But I know an unfair fight when I see one. So now I'm on your side!"

Olivia gave a shaky grin.

"Well, good. That might even things up a bit."

Almost immediately they were set upon by another couple of men, and then a few seconds later by Mordred, who made a fierce thrust at Olivia's shield.

"Mordred, you little tyke!" shouted Gawaine. "What do you think you're doing? You're on *my* side! Brothers fight together!"

Mordred looked startled, and pulled back. He stood for a moment, as if not quite sure what to do. Then, with an extremely sulky expression on his face, he half-heartedly started to help Olivia and Gawaine. It wasn't long, however, before he managed to get himself hit on the head by the flat of someone's blade.

He sank to the ground immediately and crawled into a bush to avoid further fighting.

***

Max had felt the magic on Gawaine unravel, and watched with satisfaction as the knight's blank look faded, to be replaced with his usual alert and shrewd expression. But there had been no time to watch what Gawaine would do next. He needed to find Morgana. He needed to try and neutralise any magic she might throw at the fight. He needed to make sure she didn't find the king.

As he carefully edged his way around the fighting, he noticed a small sparrowhawk perched on a tree branch above him. It was looking at him with one fierce yellow eye, and as he stopped, it flew down to his shoulder and put its beak close to his ear.

"Can we get a little further from the bridge, Max, before I transform? We're really rather closer to the Lady's island than I'd hoped to be when we had this final showdown."

"Merlin!" said Max. "Troll's toenails, I'm glad to

see you! I thought I'd have to deal with Morgana on my own!"

"Very brave of you to even think of trying, Max," said the hawk. "But I think it will need both of us. Morgana is a formidable opponent."

Max ducked into the trees with the hawk on his shoulder, and tried to get closer to Morgana without being seen. Morgana was standing a little apart from the fighting and talking urgently with Sir Richard Hogsbottom, who had made his way over to her while carefully avoiding any fighting.

Max stopped, just hidden from them by a large oak tree, and, with the slightest shimmering in the air, the hawk disappeared and in its place stood Merlin. He had his sword strapped on, and was wearing a long travelling cloak, and he looked, as usual, like a capable, sturdy knight. But Max knew that this was one fight where sword skills would be pretty much useless. Which was just as well, really, he thought with a grin, as his own sword skills were pretty much non-existent. And with that thought, he realised that he didn't actually feel scared at the prospect of facing Morgana. He felt excited, and glad that the king finally knew the truth about his sister and that now, one way or another, she would either win or be defeated.

He glanced up at Merlin, and Merlin smiled and nodded. He, too, looked glad to be facing a straightforward fight. He held up one hand and watched Morgana for a few seconds. She looked like she was getting ready to enter the fray with a few well-chosen potions and powders. Her magic, unlike Merlin's, was always encased in spell objects or bottles.

"Max," Merlin said, in a low, urgent voice. "It's time. Morgana is a very powerful sorceress. She may fight, but she may also flee, and if she does we must be ready to follow her wherever she goes. Keep close to me – I'll make sure you aren't left behind. And when we face her, remember we are not trying to kill her. I doubt if, even together, we could. We are trying to contain her, to cage her magic, to stop her being able to act in the world. Bend your magic to those ends, and I will do the same, and together we may succeed."

Max nodded, and Merlin stepped out from behind the tree and threw a spell at Morgana as soon as he had a clear line of sight. She turned, and her face went white with shock, but she plucked a pin from her hair and broke it in one swift moment, activating a counter-spell which dissipated Merlin's magic instantly.

"You!" she said, in a voice cold with rage. "But I left you—"

"Half dead from the poison you put in my wine, my lady. But unfortunately for you, only *half* dead. And Lady Griselda Pendragon," he bowed to Max with a smile, "is an expert on the magic of poisons, and brought her considerable talent to bear on bringing me back to full health. So, Morgana, I think it's time we had a serious discussion about your unforgivable treachery."

At these words, Sir Richard Hogsbottom, who had been looking rather like he wanted to be sick ever since Merlin had appeared from behind the tree, started to gently tiptoe backwards away from the confrontation. Morgana, however, turned, and seized him by the neck of his tunic.

"Deal with the brat!" she hissed, pushing him towards Max, then she turned back to Merlin and threw a scattering of powder in his direction.

Sir Richard swallowed and pulled a bottle out of his tunic. He moved cautiously towards Max, holding the bottle out in front of him like a shield, preparing to flick its contents at Max as soon as he got close enough. Max almost laughed.

He gave Sir Richard a considering look, and then said, "Well, I seem to remember you made a good frog last time... How about another go?"

Just as Sir Richard flung the contents of the bottle at Max, Max focused on the frogspell and aimed it straight at Sir Richard's head. But neither spell reached its target, because at that moment Morgana disappeared with a loud POP and Max found himself dragged behind Merlin through what felt like a whirlwind.

***

After several minutes of tumbling through the air, Max hit the ground. When the world stopped spinning he realised he was on his hands and knees on the floor of Morgana's chamber in Castle Gore.

"Very impressive," said Merlin, who was upright, if slightly wild-eyed. "I've never known a spell that could transport so many, so far. Just as well I got my fingers to the edge of it, or you would have lost us."

Morgana looked furious. She had obviously banked on being able to leave Max and Merlin three hundred miles away, and having them here in her chambers was not remotely part of her plan. But she summoned up a charming smile, and swept a large potion bottle off the shelf behind her. It shattered into fragments on the floor and tendrils of orange steam started to curl upwards. A sickly smell began to fill the room.

"No matter, Merlin," she said, in her lowest, sweetest voice. "I'm always glad to have guests. Please – *rest* yourselves on my couch."

Max felt the orange steam curl around him like a warm blanket. It whispered in his ear that it was very late, and he was very tired... He felt heavy, his head needed something to rest on, his legs felt like they

were floating in a warm bath, gentle and relaxing...
But deep in the heart of the warm, comforting feeling
there was a slight hint of cold iron... Max's head
jerked up as he realised he was being spelled.

He felt for the magic, knowing just where to put
his energy now, knowing the shape of Morgana's spells
and the way to unravel them – but his sleepiness was
increasing, his brain was fuzzy, and his magic
seemed to be hard to reach. Max couldn't undo the
spell, and he was sinking deeper and deeper into an
enchanted sleep from which he was pretty sure he
would never wake up.

The Wardstone

Just as Max's eyes started to close, there was a loud BANG! The glass in Morgana's cabinet rattled, and the ground shivered. A dose of fierce, bright magic seemed to flow right through Max, and he opened his eyes wide, his head clear again.

"Thanks," he muttered to Merlin, who was already throwing another spell at Morgana. She was hurling potion bottles and packets and powders from all corners of the room, breaking precious-looking glass vials, ripping pieces of ancient parchment and gabbling the words of several spells at once, while Merlin looked like he was in the middle of a duel, throwing up his arms to ward off the bursts of magic that were flying in all directions while shooting a few of his own spells at Morgana. The room was full of stars, smoke, explosions of bright light, and the overwhelming hum and buzz of powerful enchantments.

Max stood, bewildered, wondering what on earth he could do to help. Morgana was white as chalk but her blue eyes were fierce, her face utterly focused. Max thought he'd never seen her look so alive. Merlin was frowning in concentration, his hands a blur and his expression grim as he warded off Morgana's spells and cast ones of his own. Suddenly one of her spells caught him off guard, and he staggered, his eyes widening. She laughed and hurled another, her laugh becoming wild, almost like a scream of triumph.

"No!" shouted Max, and threw up a spell wall between Morgana and Merlin, gasping as her magic slammed through it like a bull through a net of cobwebs. But he had slowed her enough for Merlin to recover, and together they pushed her spell aside and stood, panting, ready for the next one.

But it didn't come. Instead Morgana laughed, and disappeared with a sudden POP! Max felt Merlin reach out to grasp her as she went, and then the whirlwind threw them both up in the air again.

***

This time Max managed not to fall over when they landed. There was rough, stony ground underfoot, with a few stunted trees close by, and what felt like nothing but cold clear sky around them. Far below stood a white castle surrounded by meadows, with the sea visible to the west. They were in the mountains north of Gore, and Morgana was standing a few paces away, her back to a sheer rock face with a dark cave mouth just visible behind her. Her black hair was falling wildly round her face, and she had one hand on a huge, strangely shaped rock of dark crystal which sang with power.

"It's the end, Merlin," she said, with a twisted smile. "This place is the heart of my magic. This is where

I have gathered all my power, brewed all my most potent enchantments. You cannot defeat me here. This rock is a wardstone. It will protect me against any spell you care to throw at me." She held her arms out wide, mocking. "Try it!"

Merlin frowned, and Max felt him gather his magic and fling it at Morgana. There was a shiver in the air, a tremor in the ground, but Morgana stood unharmed. She laughed.

"You have failed, Merlin. You cannot touch me – but I... I can turn whatever magic I wish on you." Her voice cut into them like shards of ice, and as she spoke she gestured towards them both and the air exploded. Max staggered as the strong iron bands of Morgana's magic started to squeeze him tightly – but he was quicker to react this time, and he managed to shake them off after only a few seconds. As he emerged from the spell he saw that Merlin was already fighting the next one, and before Max even had time to blink, Morgana was laughing and yet more magic was soaring across the space between them.

Merlin was looking grey from the effort of fighting Morgana's spells and simultaneously trying to break the wardstone's protection. Max could feel it, a wall made up of a particularly fierce version of Morgana's cold magic pushing back against every spell they tried to cast. He wanted to yell with frustration as he shoved at it uselessly – but then he suddenly stopped, and remembered that pushing *against* Morgana's magic was always the wrong thing to do. She used your efforts, she pulled them into her own spell. All he was doing was helping her. He took a deep breath, and tried to think.

How were they going to get beyond the wardstone? How could he find a spell that Morgana could not immediately break? How could he, or Merlin, contain her, defeat her? He thought of the sleep charm she had almost defeated him with in her chamber. It had worked because it had prevented him using his own magic, left him not only unable to move but unable to think... They needed something that would do the same to Morgana – and hold her forever, not just for a few hours of charmed sleep. But they also needed a spell that would break through the wardstone's protection, or they were going to be defeated. There was only so long Merlin could continue to repell her magic before he got tired, made a mistake, and left them open to the worst Morgana could do. And her worst would be unimaginably terrible...

And then Max had it! An idea! They *could* get a spell through the wardstone – but it would have to be one that the wardstone didn't recognise as harmful. It would have to be one of Morgana's *own* spells.

"Merlin!" he whispered urgently. "We need to take one of her own spells and send it back to her. Use her magic against her."

Merlin ducked a particularly vicious bit of potion and looked across at Max, one eyebrow raised.

"It might work. I'll distract her while you do it, Max. Ready – NOW!" He raised his arms and sent a storm of enchantments at Morgana that had her staggering backwards, the wardstone humming and sending up crackling sparks into the air between them. Max felt about in the brew of magic around them and caught the edge of one of Morgana's immobility spells.

Carefully, making sure he didn't allow himself to get caught in it, he gathered his own magic and embedded it deep inside the dark emptiness around the centre of the spell. At the last moment he thought of the icespell that had encased Camelot – the spell that had caught even Merlin completely unaware and frozen his mind before he could counteract it. Working quickly, he shaped an icespell and threaded it invisibly into the heart of Morgana's own dark enchantment. Then he took a deep breath and grabbed Merlin's arm.

"Now!" he said, and felt Merlin's own magic flow through to join his. They sent the immobility spell, with its secret deeply hidden, soaring towards Morgana while another part of their minds kept up the fireworks display of magic bouncing harmlessly off the wardstone's shielding.

For a few seconds, nothing happened. Max held his breath. This had to work, it *had* to. Then, with a scream of rage, Morgana realised that the wardstone had been breached. She felt herself bound in the iron bands of her own spell, and woven deep inside it she felt Merlin's magic, and Max's. But before she could even begin to fight it, the icespell had her in its grip. Her whole body became still and cold, and the cold began to seep rapidly into every cell, freezing it to hard ice, forever.

***

Max took a deep breath and then felt his legs begin to shake. He sat down quite hard on the rocky ground, and wondered if he was going to be sick. In front of him, Morgana was encased in a slab of ice, her features barely visible beneath the frosted surface. The mountain reached above them into the blue sky and all around there was silence, which seemed to press on Max's ears.

Merlin was bent over, his hands on his knees, breathing deeply. After a few minutes he straightened and looked down at Max with a sigh of relief.

"Well done, Max. I knew it was a good idea to bring you along. I think you may have just saved us both, as well as the kingdom."

He sat down beside Max, who was still looking rather white, and put his arm around him.

"It's okay, Max. Take your time. You've probably used more magic in the last half hour than you've ever used in your life before. You are going to feel a bit strange for a while."

Max nodded, and hugged his knees. He was trying not to look at the ice-bound Morgana, but it was quite difficult.

"Is that it, then?" he asked. "She stays in the ice and we never have to worry about her again?"

Merlin looked at the stark mountainside around him. A lone eagle was floating high above them in the blue sky and the castle of Gore was a small white speck in the distance. He rubbed his chin with his hand.

"It seems a good spot to leave her. Maybe further inside that cave. In fact, the cave strikes me as a good spot for a friend of ours, Max. Someone to keep an eye on her. What do you think?"

Max looked up at Merlin's amused expression and suddenly realised who the wizard meant. He grinned.

"Lady Wilhelmina?"

Merlin nodded. "I heard recently she'd returned to Gore. Her old cave is just a few minutes away. Of course, she'll have to cart all her cauldrons up here, but I'm sure that won't take too long. It's a fine view. And a perfect size for a four-hundred-year-old dragon. I can't think of anyone Morgana will be safer with."

He gestured at the ice block containing Morgana, and it disappeared. There was a rumble from deep in the cave and Merlin grinned at Max.

"Added a bit more ice," he said. "And a few tons of granite. That and a pile of Lady Wilhelmina's cauldrons ought to keep Morgana firmly in her place."

He winked, and suddenly looked as if he'd been cured of a particularly nagging toothache. His whole face looked brighter, and more joyful. It was difficult not to feel the same, especially now that Morgana had been removed from sight. Max grinned and sat up straighter.

"So," he said, looking round at the bare mountainside and the sea glinting in the distance. "How are we going to get home?"

A Well-Deserved Feast

Sir Bertram Pendragon was starting to feel rather hot inside his armour. He had been steadily whacking away with his big sword, parrying the blows of up to three knights at once and taking the occasional hit to his shield, but although he was a valiant knight and as brave as a lion, it was beginning to get rather tiring.

"What ho, Lancelot!" he gasped, as he heaved yet

another sturdy blow at a new opponent. "How's it going your side?"

Lancelot had his back to Sir Bertram and was currently fighting off two knights, his sword a flash of silver that seemed to be in at least three places at any one time. He hardly seemed out of breath, but his hair was dark with sweat.

"I think we're in with a chance," he said, and nodded over to the other side of the clearing. "We have a new ally."

Sir Bertram turned and saw Olivia and Gawaine, who were fighting together with their backs against a large oak tree. Between them they appeared to be holding off two burly knights, with a third on his knees nearby, groaning.

"Jolly good!" panted Sir Bertram. "That should just about do it." And with a huge heave, he swept the knight in front of him straight into a tree, and whacked the other on the head so hard he crumpled into a heap on the ground. Meanwhile Lancelot had disarmed both his opponents and Vortigern was flapping and quacking in their faces so they couldn't see where to pick up their swords.

It wasn't long before all twelve of Morgana's men were bundled into a sorry-looking heap by the oak tree and Sir Bertram was carefully stacking their swords and other weapons in a pile at the other side of the clearing. Adolphus was patrolling round the huddle of men, breathing a bit of fire every now and again to keep them in line, with Ferocious sitting on his shoulder grinning at them with his sharp yellow teeth.

Mordred was sitting with his back against the oak tree looking fed up, and next to him was Jerome, with a black eye. Snotty and Sir Richard had their heads together, muttering in low voices. Gawaine was standing close by, looking slightly bemused. He seemed to be unsure of what had happened, and whether he was part of the winning side or not, now that the actual fighting was over.

"Well," said Sir Bertram, stumping over to the others after safely securing the weaponry. "Now what? Where's Max got to? And what do we do with these?"

He gestured at Sir Richard, Snotty and the others. "And what's happened to Morgana?"

"Morgana has been defeated," came the voice of the Lady from her position on the bridge. "Her magic is gone from the world. But I only felt it faintly – they must be a very long way away."

Olivia looked over, startled. "Max has defeated Morgana?"

"Merlin was with him," said the Lady, frowning. "I felt him arrive – but they disappeared almost immediately." She concentrated for a second, then nodded in satisfaction. "They are both safe. Ah, well – I suppose I'd better go and find out whether they've got any transport back..." She bustled off to the island, tying her long frizzy hair back as she went, and muttering to herself.

There was a moment of silence, broken by Vortigern, who did a triple somersault and flapped his wings happily.

"Morgana's defeated! Three cheers! Quack, quack, quack!" he shouted.

Adolphus breathed a huge celebratory gout of fire which nearly singed off all the captured knights' eyebrows.

"She's gone! Hurrah for Max! Hurrah for Merlin!" he whooped.

Olivia looked at Lancelot. She felt slightly weak at the knees, and almost sat down where she stood, but before she had a chance Lancelot had swept her off her feet and whirled her round joyfully, capering around in triumph. By the time he had put her down, breathless, Olivia had got over her shock, and could only feel a huge bubble of excitement. It was all over! They had done it! They had defeated Morgana and saved the king!

But at that thought, she stopped still.

"Lancelot!" she said urgently. "Where did Max put his saddlebag? Did he take it with him?"

Sir Bertram called over from the bridge, where he was already searching the ground for the bag.

"It's all right, he left it here. But — er — I don't suppose there's anyone here who can undo a frogspell?"

He held out his hands. In one hand was a large

dark-blue frog with regal purple spots. In the other was a small pink frog with long eyelashes.

Olivia tried hard not to laugh, but she couldn't stop a small snort escaping. Neither Max nor Merlin were here, and although Lancelot had some magic, she doubted it was enough to restore the two frogs to human form.

"Someone's going to have to kiss them both," she said brightly, and looked at Sir Bertram, who shuffled his feet and coughed.

"Well, it's – um – it's the *king*... Er – Sir Lancelot?"

Lancelot looked taken aback.

"I'm not sure...," he started.

Adolphus came bounding up and sniffed the frogs cheerfully.

"I can do it!" he said. "I'll kiss them!"

"No!" shouted Olivia, but it was too late. There was a WHOOSH!! and purple stars flew around the clearing. Two enormous dragons were suddenly facing each other, one blue and one a rather fetching shade of rose. They both looked thoroughly startled.

Olivia sighed. "Adolphus, you dozy idiot. You can only turn them into dragons!"

She stepped gingerly up to the large blue dragon and curtseyed.

"Excuse me, my lord," she said, and planted a firm kiss on the dragon's nose.

WHOOSH!!

More purple stars flew around, and there stood the king, still looking a little pale, but clearly himself. He smiled at her.

"Many thanks, Olivia," he said, looking at her warmly.

Olivia hesitated, and then gestured at the beautiful rose-coloured dragon.

"You can kiss her yourself, if you like," she said.

The king looked at the dragon with a broad smile, and gave her a smacking kiss on her long nose.

WHOOSH!!

Lady Guinevere stood there, looking as beautiful as ever, and her merry blue eyes danced.

"Well! That was an interesting experience. First a frog

and then a dragon!" She turned to Sir Bertram and said, in a confidential voice, "You know, there was a fly in the saddlebag. It was a bit of a struggle between the king and myself, but I believe in the end I had the longer tongue." She licked her lips daintily. "Very tasty."

The king laughed, and clapped her on the back.

"I let you have it," he said, with a wink at the others.

At that moment, Gawaine appeared and kneeled before the king, holding up his sword.

"I believe this is really yours, my lord," he said, in a small voice.

Arthur took the sword, and weighed it carefully in his hands.

"It is Excalibur," he said, with a dark expression. "It is enchanted to look different, but I'd know the feel anywhere. How did you come to use my own sword against me, Sir Gawaine?"

Gawaine coloured, and took a deep breath. "I am sorry for what I did," he said. "I have no idea how it... I was not... I barely remember any of it. I seemed to come out of a trance, or a dream, when we were in the middle of the fight here. I think perhaps there was a spell..."

Olivia looked up at Arthur, and her voice was firm.

"He was under an enchantment," she said. "As soon as it was lifted he started to help us. He saved my life at least three times."

Gawaine's mouth twitched.

"As did she, my lord – she must have saved my life at least twice."

"Three times, I think you'll find," said Olivia, raising her eyebrow. "And actually, it might have been four."

"No," said Gawaine quickly. "I had that one totally under control. In fact—"

"Enough!" said the king, sternly. He looked down at Gawaine, and his eyes were as cold as a clear winter sky. "Do you swear this was an enchantment? Do you swear upon your life that you serve me, and not Morgana?"

Gawaine swallowed, but he looked up at the king and met his eyes firmly. "I swear," he said.

"And I, my lord, and I," came a twittering voice

from behind him, and Sir Richard Hogsbottom flung himself prostrate on the ground before the king. "It was a terrible experience! I was trying so hard to fight the enchantment! I even managed to disrupt the Lady Morgana's swordspell at the crucial moment by sneezing. I am sure that it spoiled the spell enough to save your life, my lord. I am your *most* loyal servant!"

Arthur drew back from the figure on his knees in front of him, and looked around, his expression suddenly weary.

"Sir Gawaine, I believe and forgive you," he said. "These others – Sir Richard, his boy, his ward, Gawaine's brother Mordred – I shall consider. Morgana is gone. Perhaps we should put it behind us, and start afresh."

Olivia was outraged. "But—" she started, but the king raised his hand.

"Please, Olivia," he said. "Morgana is – was – a powerful person. I was loyal to her for many years. Can I punish others too hard for being taken in by her when I allowed myself to be fooled for so long?"

"You are most wise and gracious, my lord," said Sir Richard, getting up from the ground and dusting down his robes. "Please – anything I can do to show my loyalty... Whatever small trifle..." He backed away, bowing, and bumped into Snotty, who was standing crossly behind him, not even trying to look sorry, his hands clenched and his face full of rage.

"Bind them with the other knights, for now," said the king, and Lancelot and Sir Bertram bowed, and moved in towards them.

But at that moment there was a huge roar from above, and they looked up and realised that an enormous green dragon was hurtling down towards the clearing like a mountain falling out of the sky.

***

Lady Wilhelmina, being four hundred and forty-three years old, was extremely large and very fast. After inspecting the cave and pronouncing it just right for her cauldron collection, she had graciously consented to take up her post as warden of the ice-bound Morgana le Fay. But she had agreed to return Max and

Merlin to the island first, doing so in fine style.

When they finally skidded to a halt in the middle of the clearing, Max could see the others all staring open-mouthed. Then Olivia raced towards them and flung herself at Max.

"You're all right! Max! You did it!"

After that there was universal joy and jubilation. Merlin went straight to the king, and embraced him warmly, while Arthur laughed, and winced, and protested that he was fine, and introduced Guinevere. Lancelot saluted Merlin with his sword, and was embraced in his turn, while Sir Bertram cheerfully punched everyone on the shoulder and sent most of them staggering.

Max thought he might never recover from the number of times he was slapped on the back by Sir Bertram and Lancelot. Even Arthur squeezed his shoulder tightly as he gave his heartfelt thanks — although Max thought that this might have been partly to help the king stay upright. Arthur was beginning to look slightly green by that stage, and it wasn't long before he gave up trying to stand and sank thankfully onto a couch that the Lady provided.

Meanwhile Max was bowled to the ground by Adolphus, who charged into him whooping loudly, and then bitten on the ear affectionately by Ferocious, who had immediately transferred from Adolphus's shoulder to Max's as soon as he saw him. Olivia thumped him several times on the arm till he wondered if he would ever have feeling in it again, and finally Gawaine came up and shook his hand.

"Well done, young Pendragon," he said. "I believe I have you to thank for taking the enchantment off me."

Max nodded, and grinned at Gawaine. He felt ready to be friends with anyone and everyone – it was such a relief to have stood up to Morgana and actually survived. Better – to have helped get rid of her forever. He glanced across at the other side of the clearing, where Sir Richard, Snotty, Jerome and Mordred were firmly bound together with Morgana's knights, and he couldn't help feeling even more triumphant at the expression of cold rage on Snotty's face.

"So," Max said cheerfully. "Isn't it about time for a feast to celebrate?"

"That would be good," said Olivia. "Where's Merlin when you need him?"

They looked over to the bridge and saw that Merlin and the Lady were deep in conversation. They looked rather like they were having an argument, but also as if they were very glad to see each other.

"Actually," said Max happily, "we don't need Merlin for this one." He pulled a small grey stone out of his pocket. "I've learnt how to undo Morgana's magic – and this is Sir Peverell's feast that she turned into a pebble. Roast boar's head, anyone?"

The Festival
of Chivalry

Olivia had given up raising her eyebrows and snorting at the number of knights they met who instantly fell in love with Guinevere.

"She's worse than Lady Alice the Fair, in Gore," she'd complained to the others, but Max rather liked Guinevere, and thought she was a lot more fun than the simpering Lady Alice. Lancelot had just smiled crookedly and said that he was still waiting for her to give him a proper apology for throwing his sword in the moat. And Gawaine, Olivia was pleased to note, was completely impervious to Guinevere's charms.

"I prefer girls who know how to use a sword," he had said, with a wink, and Olivia had blushed.

Now they were back at Camelot, where the castle was buzzing with preparations for the postponed Festival of Chivalry. Arthur had announced that the remaining events would take place in a week's time, to give him a chance to recover and the castle kitchens time to prepare the largest feast the kingdom had ever seen.

Olivia was disappearing somewhere almost every day, and when Max asked her what she was up to, she just tapped her nose and winked, and said that it was to do with a promise Lancelot had made her while they were on the quest. This meant that, for Max, the week of preparations was rather dull. Even Merlin was busy arranging a special display of magic and fireworks for the celebratory feast, so there were no magic lessons. In the end, Max got so bored he turned himself,

Adolphus and Ferocious into ducks, and they spent a number of enjoyable hours chasing fish in the moat with Vortigern, and playing 'Who Can Cadge the Most Bread from the Castle Kitchens'.

The one other bright spot in the week had been the banishment of Sir Richard and Snotty. Arthur had officially pardoned Gawaine, and also Mordred, who'd not had much to do with the plot at all – but Sir Richard was not so lucky. Jerome had been sent back to his family in the Welsh marches, and Sir Richard and Snotty had been banished to the furthest outpost of the kingdom – a cold, rocky island off the northern coast, with a grim stone castle and nothing but seabirds for company. Max and Olivia had gone to see them and their armed escort off on their journey north and had delighted in waving cheerily at Snotty as he stomped off carrying his bags. He was looking completely furious and snapping at his father, who was doing his best to appear innocent and misjudged. Just as they passed under the castle gatehouse, Sir Richard had given a high-pitched yell, looking around in outrage. Ferocious told them later that he had managed to get close enough to give him a sharp nip on his velvet-clad backside.

Now, however, the festival was about to begin, and the castle was an altogether more interesting place to be. It was decorated with flags and bunting and there were brightly coloured tents and campfires and horses and other animals scattered across the surrounding meadows. There were stalls selling beautiful and exotic trinkets from all corners of the kingdom, jugglers and acrobats, bards with new and fantastic tales, and travelling wizards with strange and impressive spells to show off. Excitement was in the air and everyone appeared to be in a good humour.

The day announced for the Festival dawned bright and clear. The king had withdrawn from the Knights' Cup, as he was not completely fit, but Sir Gawaine had been allowed to keep his place in the first half. Lancelot was also standing in the lists, with Olivia as his squire, ready to take on the knights who had been drawn for the second half.

The crowd was enthusiastic, and greeted each new pair of knights with enormous cheers and whoops, roaring in approval whenever any of them managed to disarm his opponent. After a morning's hard hand-to-hand combat, however, it was clear that there were really only two knights in the running for the Cup — Sir Gawaine, who had fought like a lion and bested four knights in a row to win the first half of the draw, and the newcomer, the Knight of the Lake, who had coolly disarmed every single opponent within five minutes of each fight starting.

As the time of the final approached, Max could see money rapidly changing hands among the spectators, and there was an increasing buzz of excitement and speculation about who would win. Sir Bertram had put ten gold pieces on Sir Lancelot, remembering to call him the Knight of the Lake, and was standing at one end of the castle green with his hand on Lancelot's shoulder, giving him the benefit of some last-minute advice.

"Want to hold back, keep defensive," he was saying. "Got good footwork, Gawaine, really excellent —

but he's weak on his left side, and he's impulsive. Hold off, let him make a mistake, then – wham! – in there and get his sword off him!"

Lancelot nodded gravely, the expression on his face watchful and shrewd as he eyed up his opponent. Gawaine was smiling and bowing to the crowd, and waving his sword around with a flourish, but his eyes, too, were on his opponent, and his expression was wary.

Olivia threw herself into the seat next to Max and let out a huge breath.

"Well, he's all armoured up. Let's hope he can do it."

Max nodded. Ferocious was sitting on his shoulder, watching, and Adolphus was craning his neck over the heads of the crowd to try and see what was happening.

"Are they fighting yet? Has he won? Should I help?"

"Please don't," said Ferocious, rolling his eyes. "They're both bound to end up burned to a crisp and then they'd have to give the Knights' Cup to a brainless dragon. Not exactly what it's meant for."

Olivia was sitting on her hands and biting her lip as the two knights strode to the centre of the castle green, to a roar from the crowd. She could see the king and Guinevere in the Royal Box, Arthur's blue eyes sparkling while Guinevere covered her face with her hands.

"He's beaten Gawaine before," said Max, looking at Olivia's anxious expression. "And that was against Excalibur. He's bound to win."

"Yes – but Gawaine was under an enchantment, remember," said Olivia. "He wasn't himself at all. I've seen him fight since then and he's really very, very good. It's going to be close."

It was indeed close. The knights circled each other for what seemed like ages before Gawaine finally decided to make the first move. He darted at Lancelot, who parried expertly, and Gawaine jumped back to avoid the return blow. After that they went for each other. The crowd hardly made a sound – the blows fell so fast it was almost impossible to tell who was striking whom, and there was no chance to cheer when one of them made a hit because the blow was immediately returned, and harder. Max could hardly bear to watch — he couldn't quite believe either of them was still standing. He was just at the point where he would have been happy to give Gawaine the victory if it meant they would just stop, when there was a collective gasp from the crowd and one of the knights fell to his knees, his sword arcing across the green with a flash of silver.

"Who is it, who is it?" cried Olivia, her fists clenched, as she peered into the middle of the green. There was a pause, and then a huge cheer as the standing knight removed his helmet. It was Lancelot, his hair drenched with sweat and his face bright with triumph as he waved his sword high in the air.

***

They hardly had time to celebrate Lancelot's victory before it was time for the final event of the Squires' Challenge, and Olivia was forced to set off to join the other squires, looking ever so slightly green. Just before she left, Lady Griselda appeared and gave her a hug, and whispered something in her ear. Olivia's eyes widened and she gave her mother a delighted look, and then headed off looking altogether more jaunty.

Sir Bertram frowned at his wife. "What was that about, Griselda? Hope you've not put the girl off?"

Lady Griselda smiled, and raised her eyebrows. "You'll just have to wait and see, my dear," was all she said, before settling down next to Max and patting Adolphus on the head.

"Do you think she's got a chance?" said Max to his father. Sir Bertram stroked his moustache.

"I don't know. Mordred's bigger and stronger and – well, really, Max, I have to say – he's a better swordsman. But you never know. You never know."

Max nodded, and crossed his fingers. Winning meant so much to Olivia. He really hoped she could pull it off. And then he saw Lancelot standing by the edge of the green, watching the squires. Lancelot caught his eye, and winked, and Max suddenly thought about all those days Olivia had gone off mysteriously on her own.

"She's been practising!" he said, with rising

excitement. "Lancelot's been teaching her his disarming techniques — that's what he promised her when she lost against Mordred on the quest!"

Sir Bertram brightened. "Well — that might do it. That might do it indeed." He stood up, and bellowed at the top of his voice. "Olivia! Olivia for the Challenge!" and he waved happily at her and punched the air.

Olivia smiled nervously, and gestured at him to sit down, but there was no stopping him now, and soon Adolphus had joined in.

"Olivia! Olivia! Hurrah! Three cheers for Olivia!"

Their cries were lost in the general roar of the crowd as the squires stepped forward onto the castle green and were paired off according to their place so far in the rankings. Olivia and Mordred were closely matched at the top, and everyone knew that the overall winner would be one of those two. Everything depended on the single combat.

Sir Gareth held up his sword, and the crowd hushed.

"Ready?" he asked, and the squires all nodded.

Mordred was looking grim, and Olivia was looking nervous but determined.

"Let the fight begin!" he shouted, and brought his sword slicing down through the air. There was a moment's pause, and the squires stepped forward.

There was a great deal of hacking and parrying and dodging among the other squires – but Olivia's fight ended almost before it had begun. Mordred stormed forward and threw all his weight behind a heavy blow at Olivia's shield, which she neatly sidestepped, and the next thing he knew, his sword was several yards away and hers was at his throat.

"But – what?" he spluttered.

"Sorry. Looks like you've lost," said Olivia airily. "Just not up to it, Mordred, that's all. Need a bit more practice, I'd say."

He went purple in the face with rage, but there was nothing he could do about it. Sir Gareth stepped forward and raised Olivia's arm in the air.

"Our new champion," he shouted loudly. "Lady Olivia Pendragon wins the Squires' Challenge."

***

The feast was as magnificent as any Camelot had ever seen, and Merlin's display of magic and fireworks was breathtaking. Merlin himself had set it all off and then disappeared, but not before saying goodbye to Max and Olivia.

"I'm off for a well-earned rest," he'd said, his eyes bright. "I promised the Lady I'd go and spend the winter on the island, now things are safe – but she agreed I could come back to teach you, Max, so I'll be seeing you again soon."

As the last of the amazing fireworks died away, Arthur announced that Guinevere had agreed to be his queen, and there was much cheering and congratulations. Sir Lancelot was admitted to the Round Table, in recognition both of his faithful service to Merlin, and his magnificent victory in the Knight's Cup. And Gawaine made up for his disappointment in the single combat by winning The Knight Who Can Quaff the Most Ale in a Single Swallow. Sir Bertram was quite happy to grant him the honour, since he was now The Only Knight Whose Daughter is a Squire.

There was much more entertainment to come, from the winners of the bardic competition and the many visiting jesters, as well as endless puddings and pastries, but Max and Olivia sneaked off early. They headed out into the bright moonlight and went to lie on the grassy bank by the moat.

"So – you're going to be a knight," said Max, lazily chewing a piece of grass and watching the stars above them.

"Yes," said Olivia happily. "But I knew I was going to be, even if I lost. That's what Mum said, when she whispered in my ear. She said she could see I was never going to make a lady, and if I was going to insist on spending all day getting muddy and wielding a sword, I might as well learn how to do it properly."

"Good old Mum!" said Max. "I knew she'd come round to it in the end."

"What a summer, eh Max?" said Olivia, with a contented sigh. "We've got rid of Morgana, you're going to be a wizard, and I'm going to be a knight. It's hard to believe."

"Well, don't get too excited," said Ferocious, poking his head out of Max's tunic. "You're not there yet. Couple of Max's famous wonky spells, a bit of wild swordplay from Olivia, and a few bright ideas from Adolphus and we could all still end up at the bottom of the moat with a killer pike about to swallow us whole."

"Quack! I'd save you! Quack!" came a voice, and Vortigern flapped down to join them.

"Oh good!" said Ferocious darkly. "That's okay then. That's set my mind *completely* at rest."

Adolphus raised his head happily and blew a huge spout of flickering orange-yellow flame up into the sky. Bright orange sparks floated down around them and sizzled as they hit the grass.

"It's going to be fun! All of us together! Adventures and magic and breathing fire!"

"And bread!" said Vortigern. "Don't forget the bread!" And they all laughed.

About the author

C. J. Busby lived on boats until she was sixteen, and remembers one terrifying crossing of the English Channel in gale-force winds, when her family's barge nearly overturned. She spent most of her childhood with her nose in a book, even when walking along the road. Luckily she survived to grow up, but she still carried on reading whenever she could. After studying science at university, she lived in a South Indian fishing village and did research for her PhD. She currently lives in Devon with her three children and borrows their books whenever they let her.

Don't miss Max and Olivia's first hilarious adventures!

For more thrills, spills
and spells, visit:
www.frogspell.co.uk